REBEL YELL

The Austintacious Quartet

Ostentatious but gracious

BOOK II

REBEL YELL

June, July and August of 1968
West, South & Lost

by
l.k. siga & Barbara Light Lacy

Rising Times Books
A Division of Golightly Publishing

ISBN13: 978-0-9617721-8-5 (paperback)
ISBN13: 978-0-9617721-9-2 (eBook)

Published in the United States by Rising Times Books, A division of
Golightly Publishing

P O Bos 181533
Dallas, Texas 75218-1533

Visit our website at risingtimesbooks.com or austet.com

Publisher's Cataloging-in-Publication Data
1. Nineteen sixties – Fiction. 2. Austin (Tex.) – Fiction. 3. University of
Texas at Austin – Fiction. 4. Counterculture – Fiction. 5. Hippies – Fiction. 6. Underground economy – Fiction. 7. Marijuana smuggling and
trafficking – Fiction. 8. Hippie capitalism – Fiction. 9. Austin music
scene-Fiction 10. Scuba diving--Fiction   11. Maya mythology—Fiction 12.
Young/new adult

L.K. Siga; Barbara Light Lacy

Cover Design by Scarlett Ray

Picture of the house at 19th and University, Austin, Texas, used with
permission of Patrick Uhr.

For information about permission to reproduce selections from this book,
write to Permissions, Golightly Publishing, P. O. Box 181533, Dallas, Texas
75218-1533 or email contact@risingtimesbooks.com.

First Edition: July 2013.
10 9 8 7 6 5 4 3 2 1

Chapter One

Tres said, "So what was Mona really, Gram? I mean, you don't expect me to believe she was a ghost, do you?"

Jen leaned back in her bentwood rocker and said, "Those are two good questions, Tres, two very good questions." Next Jen looked down at what she was holding in her hands, a weathered black-and-white snapshot with curled-up corners. The snapshot was from the first set of photos ever taken of her rock band The Psychedelic Crabs. The photos had been taken by Jolinda Biggs in the spring of 1968. The snapshot that Jen was holding showed head-and-shoulder shots of the rock band's five members in the living room of the 19th Street house. They were seated on their faded red couch against a backdrop of a 4'X6' United States flag nailed to the wall: Jen on the left next to Jack, then Jack's cousin, Michael A., Natasha and Taj. The far right side of the photo was fuzzy and out of focus but both Tres and Jen could make out what appeared to be the head of a young woman. Eventually, Jen took off her granny glasses and looked at Tres. Their eyes met briefly before Jen sighed and looked away to say:

"I don't really know if that's a woman in the photo or if it's some sort of glitch or other aberration due to the photo's age. I haven't looked at these snapshots in at least forty years. Maybe it's the being we called Mona, maybe not. Maybe she was just our collective hysteria—who knows? At the time we all believed in her. We called her a ghost, a 'haint' because at that time we'd been told a ghost story about a young woman who'd lived in the 19th Street house, a tale about a woman named Mona *who committed suicide in the house at the end of World War I. Those of us in the band believed in Mona's existence in different ways. None of us of course had the opportunity to know Mona very well . . . she was female, that much I believe, a woman of mystery. She seemed to come around when she wanted, usually when the band practiced . . . even all these years later I've yet to encounter anything else like her. Back in 1968 she certainly wasn't like any other woman I'd met, that's for sure."*

Jen now made eye contact with her grandson because she felt a yearning to see his father's eyes. Also, Jen had come to realize how much of his grandfather's personality had resurfaced in Tres. Jen was thinking of this when Tres said:

"It kinda sounds like Mona was in the band."

"She was, I guess, but only when we practiced. You see, almost all of us lived on the second floor and we'd practice down on the ground floor. From the very beginning Mona showed up at all the practices . . . and we felt that she helped us make music."

"You mean she taught you guys stuff?"

"Definitely. Mona mentored me into finding my voice same as Janis had. I could never have made it as a rock singer without either of them."

"That's riiight"—nodding—"you knew Janis too, didn't you?"

"Sure did. A helluva broad. So was Mona when we knew her. She was"—hesitating—"a presence in all our lives." Jen smiled her perfect smile next and got a dreamy look in those still bright sapphire eyes of hers as she thought back on those rising times. "Mona was our muse. A muse for a silver-tongued devil, a pleasant presence, a confrontational revolutionary, a fiercely independent James Dean cowboy type and—"

"You're still 'That girl can sing' according to The Austin Chronicle."

"Yeah, Michael A. stuck me with that one after I found my voice—but I can also play a decent rhythm guitar, and once in a while Jack and I even pull off a few decent double leads. I wasn't just another pretty face with a sweet voice . . . and our music was just that: our music. It was the sound of who we were and who we wanted to be, what we believe in and strive for—one planet, one world!"

"Wow, Gram, you're still passionate about it, aren't you?"

"Darned right I am. It's not just in my blood, it's what keeps my blood warm and running."

"How come music was such a big deal back then?"

Jen paused and gave the question some thought. "Well, it could be said that back in the '60s music was our collective voice, maybe even our heartbeat. It was ubiquitous. Everybody had a radio or stereo. Heck, a radio, stereo or jukebox was always playing wherever we were. We liked music so much we became like a nationwide chorus—we sang along, tapped our feet to the beat, bobbed our heads to it. And when the Beatles came on the scene there was a primal evolution, an electric revolution. The Beatles haaad IT! Man, did they ever have IT! Folk music and top forty radio had to shed their skins for the Rising Tide that was us baby boomers. It was 'evolve or devolve.' We baby boomers were so conditioned to being consumers that you might say music was our Frankenstein, a monster that we were sewing together out of dead body parts and"— laughing—"suddenly our Frankenstein was alive, it was aliiive. "

Tres said, "And there was plenty of sex, right, Gram? Free love?"

"Yesss. Life's a live-and-learn experience so we were in heat all right. We were puerile, pert and nubile—we were crazed. For us the Language of Touch was loud and profane, sweet and elegant, sweaty and"—sigh- ing—"just plain dreamy. Pleasures of the flesh will always have a voice."

"Riiight, but you guys believed in adoption and Zero Population Growth and were thoughtful about getting educated in the midst of an abstemious plethora of propinquity."

"Whoa! Big words, even for a college kid."

Tres grinned. "You paid for 'em."

Jen grinned back. "Worth every penny too."

"So get to it, please. Tell me about the summer of 1968."

For what seemed like an interminably long time Jen said nothing, merely looked out the window. There was even a moment when Tres wondered if she might cry. Finally, while still peering through the window, she said, "I see the summer of '68 as being the best and worst of summers. It was certainly a wild and woolly season, a time of drifting wood and cruising for burgers and making bubbles. A time when two of us learned the land while two others learned the sea—and one of us

3

nearly went nuts before happening upon the Crown of the Continent and climbing up Strawberry Hill . . . and all of us went down on the Hill on the Moon . . . ultimately, in the end we all came back to Austin, of course." Jen then had to pause before saying with a catch in her voice, "The worst was the loss of loved ones."

Shifting direction, Tres said, "But first tell me when it was that you yourself actually became aware of the '60s? Was it when JFK was assassinated? Or when JFK became President? The Cuban missile crisis in 1962?"

Jen turned from the window and smiled faintly at her grandson. "You certainly are a chip off the old block, aren't you?"

"Yes, ma'am."

Then without even pausing to reflect Jen said, "You know what? I've always felt that the '60s began for me when I first heard of Vietnam . . . also when my father pulled the rug out from under me the first time."

. . .

Jen told Tres it happened on a Monday. It was dinner time in their white frame rent house on the dusty street in the small town northwest of Fort Worth where Jen's mom and dad had been born and raised. To Jen her parents were as Texan as pecan pie. She thought Mom could have played June Cleaver in *Leave It to Beaver* and her dad Robert Young in *Father Knows Best*.

Though it was only a month into spring, it was hot and they had no air-conditioner. What they did have sat in the den's lone window, a rusty rattletrap swamp cooler that Dad called a "consarned contraption." The family of three was seated around their Ethan Allen dining table in the corner of the den and, like most of their dinners, little was said that wasn't prompted by a parent. The meal fare was bottom round steak fried and served with white gravy, mashed potatoes and a can of English peas. Jen should've known something was up when Dad finished eating but didn't leave the table to get a better look at the evening news from his easy chair. Dad did cuss under his breath like usual whenever a passing gravel truck's two-way radio interfered with the picture on their 26-inch

4

Stromberg Carlson black-and-white television set—but he did so with his face hidden behind the *Fort Worth Star Telegram*.

And he was reading the want ads not the sports pages.

Meanwhile, in the far corner of the den the CBS Evening News was kicking off its fifteen-minute newscast by announcing they had a new anchorman who was replacing good ol' Douglas Edwards. Dad grunted but said nothing. The new anchor had a mustache and, Dad being dead set against facial hair, Jen figured that the mustache was the reason for the grunt. The new anchor's name was Walter Cronkite and his big news was that Byron White had been sworn in as associate justice of the United States Supreme Court, the first former clerk and only NFL player ever to serve on the high court. Dad didn't grunt then but he did grunt again when Walter Cronkite announced that the U.S. was sending military advisers to some place Jen had never heard of called South Vietnam.

Jen's attention soon strayed to the fact that her bedtime was nine o'clock and she had to finish her homework before she could spin any of her 45 rpm records, the Coasters "Little Egypt" being her newest acquisition. Mom also preferred that Jen watch *Leave It to Beaver* and *The Donna Reed Show* with her so Jen could get another lesson in domesticity from June Cleaver and Donna Stone about how it was a man's job to worry and a woman's chore to smooth things over.

Jen was further pressured that evening by her desire for time in front of the bathroom mirror. By now—the ninth grade—the man in Jen's life was Joe Bob Boaz not dear old dad. Joe Bob was "stud"—cool—everybody thought so, and Jen's biggest desire in life these days was to wear his class ring on a chain around her neck. Jen was sure Joe Bob's ring would look stud with her cheerleader sweater, the one she'd be wearing on game days next fall after winning a spot in cheerleader tryouts in a couple of weeks. However, Jen's face was desperately in need of attention due to a zit there the size of a volcano. Said zit had yet to clear up despite thrice daily applications of that stinky-yucky medicated goo called Clearasil.

So Jen was about to ask to be excused when her Mom, while scraping leftovers onto a plate, spoke up, saying to her husband hidden behind the newspaper, "She's a resilient child and I think we should go ahead and tell her now so she can put her life in order."

When her father did not answer right away, just lowered the paper from his face to look at his only child, Jen swallowed the last of her English peas so as not to be reprimanded for talking with her mouth full and said, "Tell me what, Mom?"

"You need to be in a better school." As usual making it sound like whatever earth-shattering decision made behind Jen's back was done solely for her sake. "So your father has decided we're moving down to Fort Worth at the end of school." Then, trying to smooth things over: "Your father says you can have your own phone and I can have a dishwasher—now doesn't that sound nice?"

Jen was dumbfounded. She wanted to cry because there went Joe Bob Boaz and his class ring. She should've known something was up because her parents had been fussing and fighting for weeks about Dad's failing concrete business and the gossipy speculation this had spawned all over town. But finally, because she was indeed resilient, Jen said:

"Well, at least down in Fort Worth the gravel trucks' radios won't mess with the television reception and we can watch the news in peace and"—smiling hopefully—"I can watch Dick Clark's American Bandstand every afternoon after school, right?"

"Of course you can, dear," Mom said.

"Can I get my braces off before my new school starts?"

"You sure can, honey," Dad said, smiling paternally.

"And since I'm shooting up like a weed can I get some new school shoes at Thom McAn's? I've about outgrown my saddle shoes."

Mom said, "Why don't we just go ahead and buy you some new pumps?"

"Great. And down in Fort Worth we get a *real* air-conditioner?"

Grinning wide now, her father said, "Now you're talking, princess. Maybe we'll get a house with *cen*tral air-conditioning—how'll that be?" Turning to his wife, he said, "Leaving this hateful little town's gonna be good for the whole family."

"Better to go out with a bang than a whimper," Mom said with a reassuring nod.

Meanwhile, the new man on the TV, Walter Cronkite, was signing off by saying, "And that's the way it is, April 16, 1962."

Chapter Two

Tres said, "Okay, the 1960s started for you when you left your small town and moved to the big city, right?"

"Right."

"What was Fort Worth like back then?"

"Hard to say," Jen said, "'cause Fort Worth was where I just happened to land as a budding youth and youthful emotions cloud a young adult's understanding of the place they have to live. Like Nacho used say, 'We don't pick the sunset nor do we choose the sunrise, we just live out our days.'"

"Caca pasa, chachalaca—we can't change the past much less predict the future."

"Such was the wisdom of that old Maya daykeeper," Jen said, nodding. "But that same wisdom also says we can 'Look to the past for lessons and look to the future for answers.'"

"So say la maya," Tres said, nodding in agreement. "I never got the chance to know Nacho but he's strongly influenced me through you guys. My favorite aphorism of his is probably 'Pride is our greatest strength and our biggest weakness.' I make myself say that piece of wisdom all the time—it helps keep me centered."

But Jen had looked away, out through the window at the world around her. "I think," she said without looking at Tres, "that the first time I saw Fort Worth as just the accidental place where I happened to land was when I left home for Austin in the fall of '65. I recall that, as

I turned off Loop 820 onto I-35 South, KXOL was playing the Rolling Stones' 'Satisfaction'..."

Memories of 1960s Fort Worth now came to her: *McLean Junior High School, Paschal High, dates to sock hops and teen canteens, movies and proms, a bus ride to San Antonio for a football game with San Antonio Lee on which she made out with Bobby Jack O'Neal. Services at Mathews Memorial Methodist Church twice on Sundays, once on Wednesday, Christian retreats to church camp at Glen Rose and groping with Norman Atnip among the dinosaur tracks there, overnight camping in tents at Amon Carter youth camp on the edge of Fort Worth. Birthday parties for the rich kids at Colonial Country Club's Bon Ton Room. Ranch style brick homes on big lots with sweeping lawns. Carlson's Drive-in for Texas toast at 25 cents an order, Cattleman's Steakhouse, Colonial Cafeteria, Cross Keys Restaurant, Casa Manana in the summer for musicals such as* South Pacific, Auntie Mame *and* L'il Abner. *Farrington Field off University Drive for football games and track meets, Forest Park Zoo for the giraffes and monkeys and Pete the Python, Will Rogers Auditorium for Fat Stock Show rodeos with Dan Blocker and Lorne Greene of Bonanza, Roy Rogers on Trigger and Dale Evans on Buttermilk. Cars, cars, cars. Radio stations KXOL, KFJZ, KLIF. TV stations KFJZ, WBAP, WFAA, KRLD. Finally Jen turned away from the window and said to Tres:*

"I guess you could say that my life in Fort Worth was full and sweet just like June Cleaver thought it ought to be . . . but in another way it had sort of a terrible beauty about it that tempts me to give it a harsh indictment . . . reminds me of a quote from Thomas Jefferson I learned in Dr. Pat Kruppa's history class at the University: 'We confide in our strength without boasting of it and we respect that of others without fearing it' . . . Austin, however, was a place in my life that I myself chose and most of my thoughts about it are, well, more along the lines of a romantic reminiscence."

"Well alrighty then," Tres said. "So let's get to where, when and why you started making music."

"That's easy. It was in my parents' garage soon after the Beatles were on the Ed Sullivan Show. Like I said, the Beatles haaad IT! Man, did they ever have IT! That Sunday on Ed Sullivan was the beginning of

what Jim Morrison sang later: 'Move over, we're taking over.'" Then Jen
jutted out her chin and said, "Canya dig it?"

Tres nodded and said, "The Beatles, according to historians, were
a mass hysteria broadcast nationwide on The Ed Sullivan Show on
February 9th, 16th and 23rd, 1964."

"They were the inspiration that led Jolinda Biggs and me to start an
all-gal garage band called The Skirts. We did Beatle songs, Kinks songs,
whatever other top forty hits we could put together." Jen grinned. "Like
Nacho always said, 'I may not pick the sunset nor choose the sunrise . . .
but to die some each day or live a little—that choice is mine.'"

. . .

At 12:13 a.m. on Wednesday, June 5, 1968, Robert F. Kennedy, after
winning the California and South Dakota primaries in his quest
to be the Democrats' candidate for President of the United States,
was shot by a zealot with a .22 caliber pistol in the kitchen of the
Ambassador Hotel in Los Angeles.

Like his brother John before him on November 22, 1963, RFK,
too, would die of his wounds, his death coming in the early morning
of June 6, 1968.

Jack and Jen learned of the RFK shooting in the living room of
the 19th and University house. They had switched on the Monkey
Ward's Stereo Am radio to listen to Radio KNOW so as to get an
update on Andy Warhol who had been shot two days before in his
New York City loft by Valerie Solanis, a struggling writer, actress and
radical feminist. The news about RFK devastated Jen because the
New York senator had been her hope to end United States involvement in the Vietnam War. Seeing how blue Jen was, Jack said:

"C'mon, hon, let's take a spin in the Fitty Six"—his yellow
1956 Ford pickup with a 292 cubic inch V-8 engine and naugahyde
interior. "Let's have us a picnic in our private, special place—Austin's
a-cursed heat ain't so bad down there."

So Wiley and Beep Beep—the two dogs they'd adopted from
the Austin Humane Society—were loaded up and all four beings
rode east on 19th Street to Interstate 35 then north to Capital Plaza

shopping center. Here at what Jack called a "new burger joint" they bought burgers and fries.

"Fast service," Jack said as they left the Drive Thru.

"Fast food, yuck, urg, urp," Jen said, her tone desultory.

On the ride to their private, special place—a limestone grotto on a bend in Waller Creek near Jen's old dormitory, Helen M. Kirby Hall—they listened to Radio KNOW playing Jefferson Airplane's "Somebody to Love." Once they parked at the grotto, Jack left the pickup's doors open so they could hear the radio. As the Electric Prunes' "Get Me To The World On Time" played, they went down to the grotto, Jack carrying the bag of burgers and Jen toting the leather hippie purse that she had bought from a vendor down on the Drag. Both wore Levi cutoffs, T-shirts and Maya sandals.

Just as Jack had hoped, it was cooler in the grotto and while the dogs reconnoitered, Jack and Jen sat as they usually did: side by side next to the dry creek bed on a concrete bench that was a memorial to a daughter lost to polio in 1952. Jack took out their food from the white paper bag with the funny gold and orange logo on it and unwrapped his burger. Jen, however, just sat there, staring at a nearby bee as it flitted from flower to flower. Speaking more to herself than Jack, her tone still desultory, she paraphrased Nacho, saying:

"RFK could have been the bee who pollinates the flowers."

Jack said nothing, just bit into his burger—only to wince with disgust. "Lawsy merrr-cy! Ketchup on a hamburger? No way this new McDonald's place is gonna make it in this part of the world." Biting into a McDonald's french fry, though, he said, mouth full, "But their fries ain't half bad."

A pause now ensued as Jack finished off his lunch while Jen merely sat cross-legged and listlessly bobbed her right foot to no particular beat. She paid little notice when Wiley, a brown male, and Beep Beep, a white female, chased a squirrel up an oak tree about six feet away. As the dogs excitedly circled the tree while yipping and yelping, making futile attempts to get at the squirrel, Radio KNOW played Neil Diamond's "Girl, You'll Be A Woman Soon." When Jack finished eating he went over to the oak tree and Wiley and Beep Beep halted their squirrel chase to sidle up beside him and squat on their haunches. Jack then leaned his back against the oak and took out his Case pocket knife to begin cleaning his fingernails.

Jen, meanwhile, still mum and glum, reached into her leather hippie purse, past her Evening In Paris and White Shoulders perfume bottles, and took out an heirloom from her mother—a hair brush. As she began brushing her long brown hair the Jefferson Airplane's "And I Like It" came on. Jack now put away his Case knife and jammed his hands into the back pockets of his cutoffs. Still leaning back against the oak—one of his James Dean poses—he watched as Jen brushed her hair with practiced strokes. Her foot was still bobbing up and down as she was staring down into the only pool of water there in the otherwise dry creek bed. Jack watched as Jen held up her wrist to look at the chicken bone bracelet that the blues singer had given Jen at the Psychedelic Crabs debut.

But Jen was not an altogether lost soul there in the grotto; she was still aware of her man . . . and, like her mom had said back in 1962, she was resilient.

When Jack showed his uneasiness by grunting, Jen looked over at him. By now in their relationship she had learned some of Jack's body language. If his thumbs were hooked in his front pockets he was pensive and silent yet relaxed, poised—studying a situation. But if, like now, his hands were jammed into his back pockets, he was unsure and frustrated.

Now the music was Mose Allison doing "Summertime."

Jen knew the Austin heat was wearing Jack down, that he could not abide the high humidity. Jack was from the Big Bend and, though the "Big Empty" as he called it, had higher temperatures, the desert heat out there was drier and its nights thirty degrees cooler than the day. Once the Austin heat had taken hold in mid May, Jack and Jen had sought out air-conditioned structures such as movie theaters as much as possible. They had also tried immersing themselves in Lake Travis, Lake Austin and Barton Springs' cool waters and they had had evening excursions on Town Lake in Jack's Maya dugout. At night they sprinkled their water bed's sheets and

13

had even disconnected its heater. But they would still be awakened by the grungy feeling of their own sweat. So it was no surprise when "Summertime" ended that Jack said:

"Well, summertime livin' sure ain't easy for me. I can't abide this a-cursed heat much longer, Jen, I really can't. It's dad-blamed stifling. The low was just 76 degrees this morning an' it's gonna be 93 today an' they say 98 tomorrow."

By now Jen had uncrossed her legs and stopped brushing her hair. As the Fitty Six's radio played Paul Revere And The Raiders' "Him Or Me—What's It Gonna Be?" she said, "The bugs are bad too. The mosquitoes are an infestation all by themselves ... so what'll we do, hon? You got a plan?"

"Well," he said, "seein' as how the band's done for a spell ..."

"Michael A. was more than just a bass player and with him gone our little chrysalis is at a crossroads." Jen now gave Jack a look of affection. She saw that soon his hair would be long enough in front so it wouldn't escape its ponytail and could be braided. She was thinking this when Jack said:

"I wanta take the summer off, hon ... I wanta head out to the home place."

Jen pictured the Big Bend with its uncrowded beauty, and, recalling its cool nights and crisp mornings, she said, "Maybe we *cannn* pick our sunrises and sunsets. In a couple of weeks let's take a spin in the Fitty Six and have us a summer vacation at Rancho Quien Sabe."

"Ohhh, I dunno, Jen. The home place's never had electricity and it's always been run as a cold camp. What's more is that it's been sorely neglected since Granpa passed on ... it might be kind of a rough go for a—"

"Awww, all that little adobe house probably needs is a woman's touch." Sounding upbeat.

"You sure? It's bound to be a hardscrabble existence for a city girl."

Now Jen stuck out her chin and looked Jack straight in the eye. "Ben Jack Gage, are you tryin' to pull the rug out from under us?"

14

"No, ma'am"—removing his hands from his back pockets—"I'm your longtime man. For me it is and always will be 'You, me and *us*.'" Brightening next, he said, "The home place could be downright livable again if I can get some much needed chores of development done—it could even be a home for us whenever we wanted it." Then, as Tommy James and the Shondells' "Mirage" came on: "A course, there's bound to be days when we'll be hangin' in the wind—that's just a natural fact—but by'n large I expect the experience'll do us some justice." Next, grinning: "Thanks for goin' along, hon . . . I'll get off sco pro next fall, honest I will."

Jen stifled the urge to say "Life is compromise" and instead batted her sapphire eyes while showing him her perfect smile. "Okay," she said, "then, it's settled—I'm in and you're *onnn*, Cowboy. You, me and *us*."

Which was when, as if to seal the deal, Wiley got up off his haunches to shake a hird leg and spray the oak tree which Beep Beep then sniffed. Both dogs now fondly regarded their masters as a grinning Jack said:

"Goldurned dawgs."

And so it was agreed: the Big Bend was it for Jack and Jen in June of 1968.

. . .

On Saturday, June 8, Robert F. Kennedy's funeral was held in St. Patrick's Catholic Church in New York City. The deceased and seven hundred guests took a special train to the burial in Virginia's Arlington National Cemetery.

On that same day James Earl Ray was arrested by Scotland Yard in the London airport and charged with the murder of Martin Luther King Jr. Natasha and Taj, Jack and Jen and Jackson Lamar Brown—aka Cool Breeze—and his momma and granmomma learned this news during a memorial service for RFK at Mount Ebenezer Baptist Church. Later, after pulling into the driveway of the 19th Street house in Cool Breeze's 1956 pink Cadillac, Natasha and Taj, Jack and Jen and Cool Breeze heard from a street person called Ryder that Ray was using a fake Canadian passport. Ryder also said that Ray was carrying a pistol but did not resist arrest.

Ryder said that he had learned these details from Bicycle Annie who had heard it on KVET Radio.

. . .

On Father's Day, June 16, Jack took the letter Jen's father had mailed her just before he and Jen's mother had died and set it on what passed for Jen's boudoir: stacked fruit crates that also served as their hippie-style clothes dresser. Jack next lay down in their water bed to place his arm behind his long hair and his head against the wall. Above Jack were wall posters of James Dean with his thumb hooked in his jean pockets and Jane Fonda—and her wonderfully long legs—in her *Barbarella* outfit. Jack was admiring another poster—the one on their bedroom door of the 1967 Be In held in San Francisco's Golden Gate Park—when Jen came out of their bathroom to sit on the fruit crate she used as a seat. Jack now picked up the newspaper. He read that today's temperature would range from 74 to 92, that Austin's own Private First Class Joe Snitko had been killed in action in Vietnam and that the Texas quota for the July draft would be 695 men. But what he mostly did was watch Jen let down her long hair and comb it with a hundred strokes of her mom's heirloom brush. Seeing Jen once in her boudoir like this again caused Jack to wonder if the attraction he had for her there was so strong because he had seen his mother do so before he had lost her.

Without a word or apparently even a glance Jen ignored the letter from her father for all one hundred brush strokes. She did pick it up when she rose, though, and, holding it up, she said:

"Jaaack? What were you thinking?"

"Awww, I was just hopin' you might could get past some of your pain an' suffering over your folks' passing if you read your dad's letter."

"It would only remind me of how they died."

"Well, my folks lost their lives together too."

"In a car wreck—that's not the same."

"The way I was raised taught me that death is part of life, that it's our constant companion . . . you know, 'live a little each day, not'—"

"My psych prof called it 'closure'," Jen said, looking at the letter, "and I'm working on it, Jack, I really am."

. . .

On Wednesday, June 19, the time came to leave Austin.

In Texas, June 19 was known as "Juneteenth" because that was the date in 1865 on which the slaves learned that they had been freed. The 19th and University housemates were at home having their evening meal after attending a Juneteenth commemoration at Mount Ebenezer Baptist Church. Though Michael A. was absent, he was represented by proxy, Taj having placed the Purple Crab kite in a chair at the black church-door-turned-dining-room-table.

It was a candlelight dinner in which Taj served beef couscous and Middle Eastern Chick Pea salad. Cool Breeze was present, too. Nowadays he had a home, the pink 1956 Cadillac in the driveway from which he freely conducted business out of its trunk. Though he was no longer a guy who looked guilty, because he was inside the 19th Street house, home of Mona The Haint.

Nacho was also there, too, and it was he who began the dinner with a toast: "May this band of angels feel the Hand Behind the Wind as do His five fingers when they stir the energy that is spring-time in the Universe."

But after his toast Nacho said nary a word.

Amidst a general feeling of being on the cusp of adventure, it was agreed that both The Psychedelic Crabs and Purple People Eater Productions would go on hiatus for the summer. The profits from Purple People Eater's film showings in campus auditoriums were divvied up and Michael A.'s share was placed in the 19th Street kids' piggy bank, a three lock box with copper fittings that Taj had found in the attic.

"But Michael A.'s gone," Natasha said. "What about House Rule Number Two? 'If ya leave it, ya lose it.'"

Jack said, "You're kidding, right?"

"Yeah."

It was then agreed, at Jen's suggestion, that during the housemates' absence Cool Breeze would take care of house business and that he would collect the mail and newspaper. It was further agreed that he would also take care of the garden. Cool Breeze would look after the kittens, too, the white one Hannah and the four calicos, Hazel, Dot, Persia and Phoebe—but would not enter the house unless there was an emergency.

It was also agreed that all of the housemates would be back at the 19th Street house August 1 for the second anniversary of Charles Whitman's sniper murders from atop the Tower during which fourteen people died and thirty-two others were wounded, a day when all of the housemates had all been in the University Tower and had lost friends to such inane violence.

. . .

After the candlelight dinner and while Jen did some last minute packing, Jack read the *Austin Statesman*, the last real newspaper that he figured he would see until August 1. He was seated at the end of the black church-door-turned-dining-room-table with the floor-to-ceiling bookcase behind him. He was reading by the light of a solitary *votivo* candle atop the Stromberg Carlson television set, the candle set there by Taj to commemorate tonight's dinner. To add some symbolism to this memorable occasion Taj had taken from the White Room a gift that Nacho had presented the band a few days earlier: a terracotta statuette with a round base perhaps ten inches in diameter. Standing in a circle around the perimeter of the base were six human figurines, each about six inches high, each with arms stretched out so the hands were touching the shoulders of the figurines beside them.

In the center Taj had set the lit votivo.

Also atop the Stromberg Carlson and beside the statuette were the goldfish Thelma and Barney Lou in their fishbowl, their large eyes watching Jack.

Jack skipped over the front page save for the notice that the August 2-11 red, white and blue Aqua Fest skipper pins could be purchased for $1 and were worth $9.50 in admissions. He read the weather: 73 to 88, scattered, isolated thunder showers. Going to the arts section, he noted that the Adults Only Capri Theatre was showing *I Crave Your Body*, that Delwood Drive-in on East Avenue had *The Professional* and *The Cincinnati Kid* was playing at the Longhorn Drive in on Highway 183 between North Lamar and Burnet Road. He read that The Americana Theatre would premiere *Camelot*—and sighed because he and Jen wanted to see it. He saw an ad for Green Pastures Restaurant and sighed again because his and Jen's dream date was to go there for his twenty-first birthday. Club Saracen at 1418 Lavaca had a live band called The Mustangs while The Checquered Flag at 1412 Lavaca had Barbara Christopher and Mike Smith. The New Orleans Club at 12th and Red River had The Eternal Life Corporation and The Continental Club at 1315 South Congress had The Entertainers. Jack was feeling kind of bummed out to see they'd miss the June 28th Bob Wills gig at the Broken Spoke at 3201 South Lamar when . . .

. . . the candle began to flicker . . .

. . . and he turned to see Thelma and Barney Lou now turned around, their attention on something Jack couldn't see . . .

. . . when the candle went out.

So Jack picked up the terra cotta statuette with its six figurines in a circle of togetherness and the now extinguished solitary votivo candle in its center and took it downstairs. There he put it in its place beneath the black light down in the White Room. But before he went back upstairs he lit the candle.

Then, joking, he asked Mona if she would be so kind as to keep the band's flame going.

. . .

19

They had decided to drive at night that Juneteenth not only to beat the heat but because, as Jack put it: "It'll be just me'n you, hon, an' the highway an' the moon an' stars."

At the filling station across from The Tavern at 12th and Lamar where Jack went to gas up the Fitty Six with ethyl, he said to the pump jockey, "Lawww! Fossil fuel's 33 cents a gallon—whut's the world comin' to?"

"Goin' ta hell in a burlap bucket if ya ask me," the guy said.

At just after eleven P.M., back in the driveway of the house at 19th and University, Jack and Jen said goodbye to Cool Breeze, who told them "We cool."

Nacho, meanwhile, in faded jean cutoffs and white *guayabera* shirt and Maya sandals known as *chanclas*, had just loaded up Granpa Gage's bentwood rocker and Jack's cayuco—his Maya dugout named *Analuz*—into the bed of the Fitty Six. Since Jen had elected to leave behind her Samsonite suitcases and Jack his duffle bag, their luggage was just their colorfully woven Maya rucksacks plus their guitars and rainbow-colored matrimonial-size hammock—*hamaca*—all stowed beneath the upturned *Analuz*. Jack now called for Wiley and Beep Beep who had just finished peeing on their favorite shady oak on University Avenue. Once both dogs were by the Fitty Six's tailgate, Jack said to Jen:

"Watch, I'm gonna make 'em do their new trick." He then slapped the wooden planks of the pickup bed and said in a commanding tone of voice, "Load up!"

Nothing doing. Zero, zip, zilch from Wiley and Beep Beep.

But when Nacho, squatting Maya style in the pickup bed, said, "*Suben chuchos*," both dogs scrambled up into the pickup and lay down beside him.

"Goldurned dawgs," Jack said.

. . .

Jack gestured at the plastic Jesus affixed to the dashboard and backed the Fitty Six out of the driveway onto University Avenue saying, "That ol' daykeeper just goes ahead 'an does stuff like this to

20

me all the time. And, same as when he painted my pickup baby spit yellow, he never tells me nothin' 'til it's a done deal."

Jen grinned and said, "He's a phantom, your Maya grandfather, a phenomenal phantom." Then Jen scooted over next to Jack until there was not an inch between them. Jack turned the Fitty Six right onto 19th Street and went the few blocks west to turn north onto Lamar Boulevard. A couple of miles later, after passing the Stallion Drive-In on the left and the Chief Drive-In Theatre on their right—showing *The Great Race* with Natalie Wood, Tony Curtis, Jack Lemmon and Peter Falk—they took a left on Koenig Lane and went about a dozen blocks to the "Miracle Mile"—Burnet Road— where they headed north again.

As they drove past the Burnet Drive-In Theatre at 6400 Burnet Road, Jen saw that the theatre's marquee read *Cat Ballou with Jane Fonda and Lee Marvin.* They then drove another couple of miles to just before U.S. Highway 183 which was then the edge of town. Here Green Acres Tavern's marquee—reading *Junior and the Brats now playing*—inspired Jack to say, "The Crabs're wayyy better a band than Junior an' the Brats," and right away Jen said, "Oh hell yeah—*wayyy* better."

Next, after making a left onto U.S. Highway 183, they were heading northwest. With Radio KNOW's Jay Jackson spinning the platters—Johnny Otis's "Willie and the Hand Jive"—highway driving soon had the Fitty Six's 292 cubic inch V-8 Ford engine purring like a tiger and they roared toward Far West Texas at 70 miles an hour—even though Jen said not once, but three times, that the speed limit was 60 mile per hour during the day and 55 at night.

Maybe thirty miles later, after passing through two sleepy wide spots in the rode named Jollyville and Leander, they got on Highway 29. From here they went west via Liberty Hill, Llano, Burnet, Mason, Grit, on to Menard. At Menard they took Highway 190. They were riding with the windows still down and somewhere past the old Spanish mission west of Menard, Jack switched off the headlights to save on the Fitty Six's battery. This was when Jen rested her head in his lap and stuck her heels out the passenger side window. Realizing her bare feet now hung in a seventy-mile-an-hour wind, she wiggled her toes and said:

"Look, Jack, I'm hanging in the wind."

"Hang tough, hon, hang tough."

Just past Eldorado Jack tuned in the "X": Wolfman Jack's radio station broadcasting from a 50,000 watt radio station in Villa Cuna, Mexico. The first platter the Wolfman spun for Jack and Jen was The Byrds' "Eight Miles High." When Bobby Day's "Little Bitty Pretty One" came on next, the lovers sang along, liking it so much that they decided the band should add it to their repertoire.

From beneath the big steel steering wheel Jen studied her man in the light of the waning half moon rising in the eastern sky. She saw Jack as feeling happy-go-lucky now, like a dog running free. She felt that once her man was behind the wheel of his pickup on an open road in the wide open spaces of West Texas, Jack *was* James Dean. It thrilled Jen to see Jack grinning from ear to ear and bobbing his head to the music, saying hi to the rare oncoming vehicle by giving the "hidey-sign": raising the index finger of his driving hand from its grip on the steering wheel.

Somewhere around Iraan the Wolfman began to spin every Top Forty hit that had made it to number one in 1968. The lovers thrilled to "Hey Jude", "Love is Blue", "Honey", "(Sittin' On) The Dock of the Bay", "People Got to Be Free", "Sunshine of Your Love", "This Guy's in Love With You", "The Good, The Bad And The Ugly", "Mrs. Robinson", "Tighten Up", "Harper Valley P.T.A.", "Little Green Apples", "Mony, Mony", "Hello, I Love You," "Young Girl", "Cry Like a Baby", "Stone Soul Picnic", "Grazing In The Grass", "Midnight Confessions", "Dance To The Music", "The Horse", "I Wish It Would Rain"—and this week's number one hit, "La-La Means I Love You."

But the tune that really got to Jen that night on the highway was Aretha Franklin's "(You Make Me Feel Like) A Natural Woman."

"In a few weeks I'll be doing that song," Jen told herself, "because by then I'll *be* a natural woman." Then, picturing the little adobe that was the home place: "Or else I'll be a single woman 'cause a hard-scrabble existence might be too tough a gig for a city girl."

. . .

That evening of Juneteenth, shortly after Jack and Jen had left in the Fitty Six for the Big Bend, Taj went to the Engineering Building to wind up some loose ends. Natasha, meanwhile was in her bedroom in the house at 19th and University. She was packing for her trip when she heard a commotion on the front porch. Being alone and the dogs now gone, the noise left her leery. So it was a cautious Natasha who went into the entryway to peek through the screen door. On the east end of the front porch she saw a guy with his back to her. He had a burr haircut and was clad only in madras shorts and white low cut tennis shoes. With his feet well apart and his hands unseen but at his crotch Natasha knew what he was doing. When his rose colored glasses told her who he was, she threw open the screen door, went outside, saying:

"Stop that or you'll go blind, you ol' show dog."

Michael A. grinned and looked over his left shoulder. "I'm just taking a pee, Natasha, not what you think."

"I'll bet you're in violation of House Rule Number Three, aren't you? 'Underwear for women optional, required for men?'"

"Certainly not!" Smiling his smug smile. Then: "Did Ma tellya the army hadda let me out once I became a sole surviving son?"

"Yeah, she told us and"—tone of voice softer—"we were all very sorry to hear about your dad."

"Death happens to the best of us," he said as he finished his business, turned and came toward her.

"Jen and Jack and me and Taj went to see your mom . . . but not for long 'cause, well, you know how the church ladies are."

"Yeah. My dad always said Mom was married more to the church than him . . . something'll have to be done about Ma though 'cause ten grand in G.I. life insurance ain't enough and there's not call for a midwife anymore."

"That's right, I forgot your mom is a midwife." Then, sounding sincere: "Your mom could live here. All of us talked it over and we're okay with it."

"Check. Family first." Michael A. paused before saying, "I called Ma from the bus station but I came straight here . . . if that tells you anything."

"Sooo, uh . . ."—lowering her eyes—"welcome home."

Liking the sound of this, Michael A. said, "An' how providential it is to see you too, dar—"Then paused to regroup by wiping the sweat off his burr-cut noggin with a sweep of his hand before saying, "It's an oven out here—mind if I come in?"

"Sure"—opening the screen door—"your rent's paid up, ain't it?"

"It'll be a cold day in hell when my rent ain't paid up around here." Then Michael A. lowered his rose colored glasses and looked Natasha up and down. She wasn't wearing combat boots but Maya sandals instead and every inch of her was beauty in his eyes from her long dark brown hair down to the white peasant blouse hanging off her left shoulder and on down past her cutoffs to her long fine legs. He was eyeing her thighs when she said:

"I see you're still a bourgeois centaur, one who can stir up dynamic tension with just a look." She surprised him, though, because there was no death glare as she spoke, just a wry smile.

"Okay, okay," he said as they went inside, "I'll comply . . . but tell me . . . how's, uh, you-know-who downstairs?"

"Been quiet as a tomb down there since the band quit practicing."

"Not . . . haunted?"

"Maybe. I don't really know."

"And no band practice means no new bass player . . . right?"

"We got no band without you, Michael A."

It touched him to hear that, touched him even more to hear her say his name. Feeling buoyed by this, he said, "So, uh, what say you'n this hot hunk of a Mexamerileb spend some time together?" They were both in the entryway now, in front of her bedroom door, Natasha hesitating before saying:

24

"No thanks ... I'm going through too many changes right now."

"That makes two of us." Then, brightening: "But what's *your* story, morning glory?"

"Actually, I got no time to talk now ... see, I'm kind of in a hurry 'cause I'm going out of town."

"Oh?" Needling her with his sly grin. "Off to Peking for a meeting of the Revolutionary Council, are we?"

"Not exactly—the Struggle doesn't really need me until the end of August."

"Check. Chicago, right?"

"Yeah, I'll be in Chicago at the end of August. Definitely."

Now he looked at her feet and said, "So how come you nixed the combat boots?"

"They won't fit in where I'm going."

"An' just where are you going if you don't mind my asking?"

"A tropical island."

"Yeah, right, and I rule the world."

Wanting to change the subject, she said, "Taj kept your Triumph motorcycle maintained while you were away."

"Like I always say, 'Taj is a good guy to have liking you.'" Then kept staring at her until she caved and said:

"We need to talk, Michael A."

. . .

Around midnight that Juneteenth Taj was on the Crow's Nest part of the roof. He was dancing the Watusi while saying goodbye to the kittens when he realized that one kitten was missing—Hannah, the white kitty with an uncommon air of coolness even for a cat. Then, looking for Hannah, Taj's first glance over the rooftop gave him a start: a woman in a white diaphanous gown. She was seated atop the red brick chimney that Taj now knew led down to a hidden fireplace. Looking harder, however, Taj saw it was only Hannah perched atop the red brick chimney. Taj tried not to picture the young woman named Mona Devine who, according to Cool Breeze, had hung herself after having been jilted by a soldier. It had happened back

25

in World War when 19th and University was a house of ill repute. Mona had come up here to the Crow's Nest, put a rope around her neck, tied it off to the chimney and jumped in. The fall took her head off. When they found her, her head was on her belly. Natasha now swore that Mona lived in the downstairs bathroom and that Mona liked the music of the Psychedelic Crabs' so much she danced the Watusi from within the black curtain down in the White Room.

So, before Taj went back down into the house to join Natasha in their bed, he said a silent goodbye to Mona, too.

. . .

Tres said, "So how did Taj and Natasha get together?"

"Oh, you know," Jen said, with a quick shrug of her left shoulder, "boys and girls with adjoining bedrooms, sharing a bathroom, living and playing together . . ."

Grinning, Tres said, "Like I tolja—an abstemious plethora of propinquity."

Jen said, "Do you know what 'absurd juxtaposition' is?"

Chapter Three

Early Thursday morning, June 20, that waning half moon was now low in the western sky in front of them as Jack and Jen and Nacho arrived at the tail end of the Rocky Mountains: Alpine, county seat of Brewster County, biggest county in Texas. Jack was still driving, of course, and giving the hidey-sign to one and all. Jen was still close beside him, but now Nacho sat next to her in the cab of the Fitty Six. They had already passed Sul Ross State University on the right and now the forty-foot tall 'A' made of whitewashed stones on 'A' Mountain was on their right, Alpine's Radio KALP playing the Mamas and Papas' "Monday, Monday" as they turned south onto Highway 118, the turnoff to Big Bend National Park. On the edge of town they stopped at Aguilar's filling station for fossil fuel, beer and victuals, firewood, a case of under-the-counter Senor Fuego tequila and, of course, some gossip.

As Wiley and Beep Beep reconnoitered in preparation for nature calls and as Aguilar gassed up the Fitty Six, Jack winced thrice. He winced, first, at the price of gas and, second, at Aguilar's news say that Scooter Culero had signed up for his second tour of Vietnam. Jack's third wince was at the sight of Nacho and Jen picking tumbleweeds.

. . .

"Hoo … hoo."

"And just *who* … are … *you*?" said Jen.

"That's a Big Bend elf owl," Jack said.

As shadow emerged into substance for the dawning of summer solstice, June 21, Jack and Jen lay suspended over a field of gold 6700 feet above sea level. Their eyes were greeting a silver-lined crimson dawn in a place Nacho said was not unlike their pyramid perch last December in Palenque. As they had in Palenque, they lay in their rainbow-colored matrimonial–size hamaca. Not atop the nine levels of Palenque's "sacred living mountain" the Temple of Inscriptions, though; instead they were a foot above a patch of yellow Mexican Hat wild flowers atop a precipice near the South Rim of the Chisos Basin. Their hamaca was strung between two branches of a desert willow planted by Granpa Gage atop Jack's placenta on the day his namesake—his *tocayo*—was born.

As the Big Bend elf owl, maybe six inches high, flew away to disappear below the precipice, Jen saw two birds high above the owl launch attack dives.

"Uh oh," Jen said, no longer whispering.

"Falcons, probably Peregrines," Jack said. "They're hoping to have elf owl for breakfast."

"Such is life," Jen said. "We're all on somebody's menu."

Just then from below the precipice appeared two squadrons of monarch butterflies on their annual northerly migration from central Mexico. One squadron came to rest in the desert willow and another on the pink and yellow flowers of a nearby lantana bush. Overhead a vermillion flycatcher—as red as a cardinal but larger—began to execute graceful aerial acrobatics so as to snag its breakfast of flying insects. Smiling now, Jen, who was lying on Jack's left side, her head on his chest, diddled a Mexican hat flower in Jack's belly button. Looking beyond she could see Mexico a hundred miles east, south and west because of the Big Bend: where the Rio Grande changed from a southeasterly course as it exited Santa Elena Canyon's 1200 foot walls to wend its way northeast until it turned southeast again for its run down to the Gulf of Mexico.

Since Nacho would soon depart the Big Bend, it had been decided that the three travelers would see some countryside. So after driving the one hundred miles from Alpine the Fitty Six had been left in the parking lot near the ranger station in the Chisos Basin. From there the three travelers had hiked a dozen miles to Campsite SW-4, a place on Mother Earth that Jack and Nacho knew well: a view of the top of the world, the core of the 12,500 square miles that made up the Big Bend. It was a bird's eye view of more of Mother Earth than Jen had ever seen before.

Jen was admiring this view when up sailed a Yucatecan white straw hat from the ledge below Campsite SW-4. The hat spun in a slow arc before coming to rest in the field of gold. A giggling Jen said "purple people eaters" as a swarming squadron of purple swallowtail butterflies began to alight on the straw hat. Next Nacho scrambled over the ledge and onto the precipice like a Maya leprechaun. He spread his arms and stretched with his eyes shut. His nut brown and wizened old face was grinning, though, and when he opened his brown eyes wide he began to dance a Maya jig called "Dance of the Jaguar Warrior." Now sashaying around his hat of purple butterflies, he said, "This is a dawning that is like dreaming with your eyes open." Next he placed his right fist over his heart, thumped it once and said, "We Maya have always been here before. Forever here. Here forever. Ever forward. In this world we now visit we are but part and parcel to its dominion. Here in the Big Bend rainbows wait for rain and *el rio bravo* sights the dawn through Santa Elena's stone walls. Here the stars at night cally with the mountains that make the Great Divide and here the planet is at peace." He paused to point at Jack and Jen before saying, "Be here now, my angels—for whom do you harm? One *world*, one planet."

"Cool," Jack said. "But everybody here's havin' breakfast but us—whut we got for first grub?"

Nacho reached down and came up with the tumbleweeds he and Jen had picked the day before. "Earth food," he said.

This time it was not Jack but Jen who winced. It was Resilient Jen, though, who said, "A girl's gotta eat."

. . .

The trip was on Don Cesar Augustus Winterhalter. Also known as the Cozumel Maya daykeeper called He Who Pollinates the Flowers. Also known as Nacho.

The night of the Juneteenth dinner, before Nacho had left with Jack and Jen for the Big Bend, he had bid goodbye to Natasha and Taj by saying:

"Though I am unable to join you, it is my fondest desire that you go to Mayaluum, to that place we Maya call 'Where the Sky Is Born', our Garden of Eden, our Creation Place where every ending is a beginning. There one can look into la maya's great past for lessons to seek answers from the future. There one can experience la maya's gods—The Forces That Are. If you allow this, you will expand your horizons by broadening your perspective. Not only will you see Mayaluum's 5000-year-old culture, oldest existing culture in this hemisphere, but you will witness the wind on the water and, above all, *learn*. To learn is to love to live. Learn to see beyond normal man's clouded vision which is not unlike breath upon a mirror. *Live* on the water, *live* in the water—be*come* the water. Water is life. For as is earth and sky so is sea: one *world*, one planet . . . study Maya blue and feel *xutan*." Saying it 'shoo-TAWN.' "Ours is a cyclical journey forever revolving forward like our home the Milky Way. A journey from within which one can see 'what it was' so one can live with 'what it is' and then maybe feel '*que sera sera.*' Now go, Natasha and Taj, journey that winding, up and down Road of Self Discovery." Finally, he whispered:

"Do you know the answer to the Maya riddle 'What is a traveler on the Road of Life?'"

"Time," Natasha said.

"So say la maya and Maya karma . . . and know full well that we are all Maya in these days of rising times and future past."

. . .

Back in Austin on June 21, the sun rose at 6:29 a.m. Michael A., however, rose at 11:37 a.m. Actually, all that rose was his hun-

30

gover head and it did not rise very far. This was because Michael A. had a twinge of the misery from the beer bender he had gone on as his way of rolling with the punch Life had thrown at him: the fact that Taj and Natasha were now a couple. So Michael A. was down—face down in the remnants of an extra-large pepperoni and anchovy pizza from Shakey's Pizza at 2915 Guadalupe. Wearing nothing but his army green boxers, he was slumped in the straight back chair at the head of the church-door-turned-dining-room-table. He had opened a bloodshot eye to note that over by the Stromberg Carlson television set Thelma and Barney Lou were giving him the fisheye when he saw his reflection in the fishbowl. He did not freak out even though he saw his face was a bloody red mess.

"Kaboom," he said then slurred "Nothin' but misery an' pain" and passed out again in the pepperoni and anchovy pizza—the cause of his red mess of a face. His mind and body then dissolved into a reverie of September, 1953. It was his first day of school in first grade at Casis Elementary School and the teacher was coming down on Michael A. for cutting up in class, saying:

"Michael A.! Michael A.!" Clapping her hands loudly. "Give me your undivided attention."

Michael A. had no idea what "undivided attention" meant. So, perplexed, his face in a frown, he said, "I got no attention to give, teacher." Whereupon the rest of the class mocked his disorientation with raucous laughter and the humiliated Michael A. ran all the way home to Ma.

That day in 1953 had been his initial awareness of taking a punch from Life.

. . .

At noon, summer solstice, June 21, just before they were to hike back down to the ranger station, the three travelers stood on the precipice known as the South Rim and watched three *remolinos*—dust devils, whirlwinds—march north in single file until one veered off to the southwest.

Nacho declared it a good omen.

Then the three travelers checked again to see they had left Campsite SW-4 just as clean and pristine as they had found it.

"A good guest leaves no wake," Nacho said.

. . .

Natasha liked Chel's greeting of "Que tal" which meant "Hello, how's everything?"

It was the afternoon of Friday, June 21, summer solstice. Two of Nacho's children, Chel and his very pregnant sister Chanil and Taj and Natasha were topside on the *Zak Be* taking siestas. Chel and Chanil were astern, stretched out on the pillows of the cockpit's port and starboard benches beneath the bimini awning that shaded the cockpit. Taj and Natasha, meanwhile, were in a Maya blue matrimonial-size hamaca strung up between the main mast and the forestay and shaded by a tarp which collected rain for the 42' ketch's water tanks. Taj and Natasha were not dozing, however; instead, the lovers had hung themselves upside down in the hamaca as if to illustrate both the different perspective and the cultural jet lag that they were feeling here in Mayaluum.

It was Taj who first noted the blue-green lightning off to the west. He watched it emanate from within a small squall crossing the Cozumel Channel. As the squall made for the *Zak Be* and Taj wondered if its green lightning was part of what Chel had meant about Itzamal Reef being "a sacred place where strange forces were at work," the squall spawned four water spouts that scudded straight for the *Zak Be* to anoint her and all aboard with a heavensent rinse.

Chel proclaimed it a good omen.

. . .

It was sunset—*atardecer*—June 22, and Taj, Natasha and Chel were on the Hotel Tulan's penthouse terrace, Radio Havana having delighted Natasha with the news that democracy was emerging in Czechoslovakia. But Chel then topped that news by saying that Nacho owned the Hotel Tulan. Astonished, Natasha said:

32

"But I thought that la maya don't believe in property ownership, that they believe they belong to the earth and not the other way around."

"True, very true. But my father Don Cesar Augustus Winterhalter is a man of varying beliefs." Then: "He also owns the *Zak Be* which is where you will reside."

They were on the Hotel Tulan's penthouse terrace, a rooftop garden that took up the west side of the Hotel Tulan's seventh floor. Besides its *palapa*—a thatched conical canopy on support posts—the terrace was covered with a green sweep of manicured grass adorned with verdant green elephant ear shrubs, deep red bougainvillea and blossoming bright yellow copa de oros that were blossoming even in summer's tropical heat.

Natasha was at the far end of the penthouse terrace and had placed her hands on its balustrade to peer down at the Maya blue waters of the Cozumel Channel. According to Chel, "Maya blue" was la maya's name for turquoise, blue-green, aquamarine and it was the color of the divine. Anchored below was the *Zak Be*, the sleek white ketch that Nacho also owned and which Chel had said would be Natasha and Taj's residence here in Mayaluum. For a long time Natasha stared beyond the ketch, toward the western horizon where the east coast of the Yucatan Peninsula ran north from the tiny town of Playa Del Carmen to the nearly uninhabited sand spit of an island called Cancun. South of Playa Del Carmen was Akumal, Tulum and on down to Belize. Finally, Natasha sighed and said:

"It's like a view of heaven."

"Cozumel *is* heaven to us Maya," Chel said as he joined her. "Cozumel is said to be either the first level of the thirteen levels of Maya heaven or the first level of Maya Purgatory's nine levels. But for me it will always be Tulan, the paradise where the Maya creation myth is centered."

"Is that why Nacho calls Cozumel his 'Maya Garden of Eden?'"

"I dare not speak for Father."

"I know so little. Xutan? The Forces That Are? Maya karma?" Chel did not answer, so Natasha said, "No matter, I am here to learn.

33

All I know of Cozumel Island is what I read in the University's Main Library, that it's eight miles wide and twenty-eight miles long and was Cortez's first landfall when he began the conquest of Mexico."

"The year was 1519 and Cortez was welcomed by my ancestors the Cozumelecos. But when Cortez plundered and destroyed our temples his lust for gold was used to lure him away to prey upon our enemies the Aztecs." Chel's eyes brightened as he said, "And *that*, Natasha, is Maya karma—'treachery for the sake of revenge.' Maya Karma on the other hand—'Karma' with a capital 'K'—well, *she* is something entirely different."

. . .

To Taj and Natasha the *Zak Be*—pronounced "sock bay"—was a honey from stem to stern. From its center cockpit, streamlined deck cabin, mahogany masts, steel rigging, teak decking to the dive platform astern the *Zak Be* was a place to live unlike any Natasha had imagined. Living aboard the ketch was further proof that, as Natasha had said to Michael A. on the front porch of the 19th Street house before leaving Austin, she was going through some changes. And she was open to this.

As for Taj, he would never be the same again,

Living aboard the *Zak Be* above Itzamal Reef meant that the mainland—the Yucatan Peninsula—was to the west while Nacho's Hotel Tulan to the east dominated the skyline of whitewashed shops along *la malecon*—the levee, Front Street. North and south was the Cozumel Channel. The *Zak Be* herself was a unique room with a view, one that that changed with the wind atop its suspension on an aquamarine looking glass—the Cozumel Channel—where its mute denizens lived in a mostly coral world ensconced in white sand. A world where sound came at you so fast you did not know from which direction it had emanated. Where everything was magnified twenty-five per cent. A world where you felt the Caribbean's tropical warmth, where you lost smell and for taste all you had was the taste of salt in your double hose regulator's rubber mouthpiece.

A biosphere which Taj and Natasha yearned to explore.

It was only natural that it would be Chel who would introduce them to diving for it was he who operated the island's only dive shop, Current Events Dive & Charter. Chel described diving as the "art of dancing beneath the primordial sea to the primal rhythm. Diving is being harmonious with the current so as to feel the rhythm in your bones."

Taj and Natasha's first dive in Mayaluum centered around an orientation to their dive equipment: double hose regulator, mask and fins, a backpack to hold the air tank. Their maiden voyage was a mere five feet down to clean the *Zak Be's* hull free from the grass and barnacles that had grown there. On that dive below the hull they learned to cope with Mayaluum's current, the worldwide force known as the Gulf Stream or, to la maya, "the River of Time." They learned to use their bodies to flow with the Stream, to live within it, to respect it. They discovered the art of neutral buoyancy: the proper balance and control of their bodies necessary to maneuver with the least amount of energy and thus consuming the least amount of air. By mastering neutral buoyancy they could ascend via their inhalations and descend via their exhalations.

On their first *real* dive in Mayaluum—thirty feet below the *Zak Be* in the Cozumel Channel's cobalt-blue sky, 150 feet of visibility in every direction—they descended to a foot above the white sand bottom. From here they were following the anchor chain on a damage check when a puff of black exploded beneath them. A moment later they saw the black puff came had been expelled by an octopus as its defense mechanism of expelling black ink to cover its escape.

From then on Taj and Natasha and would refer to the Itzamal Reef dive site as "The Octopus's Garden."

. . .

On Monday, June 24, Radio Havana announced that police had raided Resurrection City, the Southern Christian Leadership Corps encampment of 2500 people established May 11 on the Mall in

Washington D.C.. Despite having a permit, 124 occupants were arrested and the encampment was demolished.

. . .

"Top . . . of . . . the . . . world . . . to . . . you . . . from . . . the . . . bottom . . . of . . . the . . . sea."

It was Wednesday, June 26, when Taj mouthed these words to Natasha as they made bubbles thirty feet down in the Octopus's Garden. Natasha's reply was to smile around her regulator's mouthpiece and give the diver's hand signal for "All is okay."

It was their tenth dive and by now Chel had shown them the diver's way well enough for Natasha and Taj to be on their own down here. Again and again their dives had been glorious. Superb and magnificent—all they ever wanted, all they ever needed. Like Jack and Jill, they had gone down the hill to fetch a pail of water, but they had come up reborn. They had skillfully left the human realm above them to descend into this nearly soundless creation that was the site of Planet Earth's first life, birthplace of humans' initial ancestors. Following decorum, they left the white sand bottom untouched and commanded their bodies to hover parallel a foot above this blanched seascape as they maneuvered in reverent respect over this ten-millennia-old graveyard, final resting place for the skeletons of billions of generations of sea life, this cemetery of billions of shell creatures who, after having had their turn in Time, had passed on, their bleached skeletons reborn as grains of sugary grit beneath the Maya blue Caribbean that floated the *Zak Be*.

Heading west, Natasha and Taj nodded politely at a nearby brain coral atop which the octopus was regarding them like an amused Humpty Dumpty. At the island's drop-off into the Cozumel Channel the divers bowed their weightless bodies and plummeted in slow motion down beside the island's drop-off, a limestone wall. At a depth of eighty feet they brought themselves parallel again so as to drift dive, be swept away on a magic carpet ride, aloft on the wings that were their lungs as well as the waterborne wind that was the River of Time. Yet they were not lost in Time. They were travelers who felt found again. They felt that life itself is a current, one bearing its precious cargo on the back of that most omniscient of The Forces That Are: time. Natasha and Taj were alien Ambassadors of Good Will from another world who said hello to their fellow travelers: they blew kisses at a stingray's down-under smile, sang to a moray eel, moved their finned feet to the beat of a kajillion million coral polyps in the wall of the drop-off, the ledges there a communal rainbow of living rock feasting on the existence that was Itzamal Reef, the cornerstone of this aquamarine delight. They measured their grace to the pulsing the beat of their being:

Inhale
exhale
inhale
exhale

This was when a pair dolphins showed themselves: a male and a female shooting out of the drop-off wall to crisscross above and below Natasha, echo-locate off her body, large smiles on their bottle-nose faces. Being an Ambassador of Good Will from another world and having become cautiously sagacious, Natasha smiled back. Taj did so, too, there being little breath on each lover's mirror to fog their vision. For, as Nacho had said that Juneteenth night they had now learned to love to live.

In this life, anyway.

Chapter Four

So there they were: South Brewster County, Northern Chihuahua Desert badlands, down along the Rio Grande, a mile south of Terlingua—Rancho Quien Sabe.

Or as Jack called it: the home place.

Jen was inside the little adobe home thinking, first, that it was hot as Hades in here and, second that the condition of the adobe brick walls was worse off than she had recalled. She was biting her tongue at the dust bunnies in the corners, the spider webs on the walls, the dirt and fresh footprints on the floor, the animal scat of varying sizes, the smell of piddle and the thick layer of dust on *every*thing.

Meanwhile, Jack was out on the front porch trying to be heard over the forty-mile-an-hour southwest wind while saying, "I know the home place doesn't appear very prosperous, Jen. But it will, you'll see. Like you said, it needs a woman's touch."

Same as the small bare adobe structure it fronted, the front porch wasn't much. There were no floorboards, only creek sand cemented solid by the desert's few rains and further packed down by the boots of whoever had walked it since the summer of 1951, when Granpa and Nacho had brought their grandson Jack here after he had lost his parents in a car wreck on U.S. Highway 67 south of Fort Stockton. The porch's shed roof, save for one piece of corrugated, bent-by-the-wind rectangle of tin left behind by a blue norther a few years before, consisted of inch wide ocotillo branches nailed to a weathered gray two-by-four. Jack, now beside the screen door that was the home place's entry, was peering up at the tin piece and ocotillo branches and saying, "See, hon, this right here's a chore of development—a new porch roof."

"Jaaack?"

"Whut?"

"There are flies in the kitchen."

Going inside, Jack saw Jen fanning away flies from a kitchen sink that had a manual pump instead of faucets. Seeing the fresh footprints on the floor, he said to himself, "Los Boys have been here." Then, teasing, he said to Jen: "An infestation of flies, huh? Just be glad we got the stinging lizards to hunt 'em down." Next, coming up beside her to open the back door so as to let some of the flies out, he said, "But never you mind about anything here inside, hon, 'cause inside's just too durned hot in the summertime—only the centipedes like it—so we'll mostly be livin' out in the kitchen patch."

"What in the world is a 'kitchen patch'?" Jen said, now looking for centipedes as she tried to work the water pump's long, rusting handle . . . but all her efforts got her was a hiss of dust.

"I'll prime that pump here directly," Jack said, and raised the kitchen window so he could shoo away the flies. Then he walked out the back door and onto a small bare patch of desert unevenly bordered by five-foot high ocotillos and shaded by ocotillo limbs lashed atop twenty-foot-long 2X4s. "*This* is the kitchen patch, hon. It's where we'll hang our hamaca 'cause it's shady out here an' has the house for a wind break. We'll cook on a wood stove that's around somewhere. We can do the laundry in the sink and hang it high same as our dry goods'n food'n other perishables so the varmints can't get at 'em. Granpa an' Granma always kept chickens out there but—"

"Chickens?" Looking at the *huuuge* pile of scat in the kitchen uncovered by the flies' exit. "Are we gonna have chickens?"

"Maybe, depends on the varmint situation, but I expect, mostly, it'll be Bonanza Beans'n Meat'n Potato Supreme'n Pan Fried Ham with Red Eye Gravy—all that good stuff." Now pondering the kitchen patch, Jack said, "I'll water those ocotillos—we call 'em a 'living fence'—an' it oughta be right pretty when—and if—the rains come along about my birthday. Hopefully a fence'll keep the varmints out."

"What varmints?"

"Humans have to share the Chihuahua Desert out here in Far West Texas, hon, an' everwhere ya look, somethin's out to get you'n yours—varmints mostly. Bears, coyotes, javelinas, ringstails'n rattlesnakes'n skunks on down to rats'n mice'n flies'n centipedes'n scorpions'n other bugs'n *toritos*'n *diablitos.*"

Jen sighed and said, "Wow, that's a lot of critters and infestation and stuff for a city girl." Then after another sigh she said, "Oh my lord and I thought my biggest problems would be the lack of electricity and running water, the wood stove, pumping water . . . and the outhouse."

"By the way, that reminds me of something."

"What?"

"Well, first off, you'n the dogs have gotta learn to get along with Mr. Bullsnake."

"S-snake?"

"Yeah. He lives under the front porch. We need him because he eats rats'n mice . . . an', uh, other stuff."

· · ·

The Chihuahua Desert was adamant, insistent that, if Jack and Jen were to work on its turf, they must wear boots. So, instead of his Maya sandals, Jack got around in his Nocona boots, a T-shirt and cutoffs—and it took some getting used to for Jen to see those long legs of Jack's running down from the cutoffs to the Noconas. For Jen it was a head scarf, cutoffs and a peasant blouse. The idea of boots was somewhat daunting for her so she wore an old pair of Noconas that had belonged to Granma Gage. Jack kept his hair up in a ponytail beneath a windbent, sweatstained cowboy hat. Jen wore one of Granma Gage's sunbonnets—but only when she absolutely had to.

Despite the dust and the wind, and the summertime heat, the Big Bend was still more comfortable than Austin's stifling humidity. As Jack had predicted, most of their time at the home place was spent in the kitchen patch. Jack nearly always sat in Granpa's bentwood rocker and Jen in the rainbow-colored matrimonial-size hamaca Jack strung up between two cedar posts. The dogs stayed in the shade, usually beneath the hamaca or, when the sun was right, in the open kitchen window. The eyes of everyone at Rancho Quien Sabe always greeted the dawn and they never missed a sunset. Days became a routine of a lazy sunrise breakfast followed by working on songs, lunch and a long siesta—and all kinds regular chores. At sunset there was always a kettle of buzzards to be seen circling effortlessly somewhere in the sky above. Dinners were at twilight. Jack was the firemaker and Jen was the homemaker. She learned to use the nearly rusted out wood stove, often while hearing Jack talk of Granma Gage, how, according to Gage family lore, she had used the wood stove to warm tortillas for Pancho Villa. The home place's food stores were never low because, besides trips up to Aguilar's in Alpine, Jack was a trader: he ferried folks across the river in *Analuz* in return for some of the victuals those folks peddled in Terlingua. Thus, jicama, chiles, fruit, tortillas, beans and rice were abundant in the home place.

Foremost among their goals this summer vacation in the Big Empty—besides their life goal of striving to improve their music—was to make the home place Mother Earth friendly. Jack soon decided that his first chores of development that summer of 1968 would be to erect a whole roof of Saltillo tiles then lay a floor of handmade and fired red clay tiles.

Jen was gung ho to help and Jack was right proud of that.

Though the cool of the evening was reserved for these chores of development, there were times when Jen would declare "all work and no play makes Jack a dull boy," and thus early in the morning *Analuz* would be paddled up river into Santa Elena Canyon, the Wonder of Nature Jack called the "Otherworld." Without exception, however, after dining during dusk, Jack and Jen would play their guitars and harmonize, often serenading Mr. Bullsnake or other critters passing by. In Jack's worldview critters weren't "varmints" unless they trespassed.

On one occasion their music so enchanted a coyote that he howled along.

Whenever the moon was full enough to illuminate the nighttime landscape with her silver mystery, Jack and Jen took hikes. Jack's feel for the nocturnal skillfully led them on these treks along the game trails. The lovers would remain mute, nonverbal, never say a word. They simply … *observed*. They became the embodiment of that Maya riddle that asks "What is a traveler on the Road of Life?" Whatever encounters with desert life unfolded were met with respectful behavior: Jack and Jen would stand silent and still, become one with the desert in their collective mind and in one voice would say to whomever they had chanced upon:

"I am Time, another like yourself."

. . .

On Friday, June 28, the day Taj and Natasha were to sail the *Zak Be* to Akumal all by themselves, Chel presented Taj and Natasha with a gift, an artifact, something old and rare and deemed sacred. The gift was the jaw bone of a baby manatee, unusual in that it was nearly round. By using the manatee's nearly round jaw bone as a perimeter, jaguar whiskers had been fashioned into a web with a hole left in the middle. Four strips of deerskin had then been attached to the manatee's jaw bone, one to suspend it and the other three on the bottom of the jaw bone had been attached so as to suspend three brilliantly bright red feathers of the resplendent quetzal, a bird held sacred by la maya.

Chel called the artifact a "dreamcatcher."

Chel said that He Who Pollinates the Flowers had asked that this dreamcatcher become Natasha and Taj's dreamcatcher and that the dreamcatcher had once belonged to a woman of practical wisdom.

Chel said, "The hole in the dreamcatcher's center allows good dreams to a sleeping soul. Bad dreams, however, are trapped in the web and perish in the light of day."

43

"Hmmm," said Natasha, "a dreamcatcher might be just what the doctor ordered."

"Or daykeeper," said Chel.

. . .

By June 28, the tropical sun had turned Natasha dark and sultry and Taj into a Pan-like creature whose head had an afro fringe resembling a golden halo.

On that Friday Natasha and Taj sailed the *Zak Be*— with twenty dive tanks aboard—across the Cozumel Channel to the mainland. This was only a day sail, no more than a few hours twelve miles west-southwest before passing through a break in the barrier reef that bordered the half-mile wide Akumal Bay. Akumal—"place of the turtle" in Maya—was a coconut plantation, a Maya village consisting of seven thatch-roofed huts called *chozas*. These chozas had been built beneath the plantation's thriving coconut palms on a white sand beach, all seven doorways of the chozas facing east so as to greet the dawn. Akumal Bay was always tranquil due to the reef that separated it from the channel. Beyond its half-moon-shaped beach and chozas—west—was the life-giving greenness of the canopied forest. Life was simple and complete for the Akumalecos: their water came from a *cenote*, a well supplied by rainwater that had percolated down through the Yucatan Peninsula's limestone base. Their base food supply came from their fruit and vegetable gardens—*milpas*—planted in cleared sections of the forest—*la selva*. They fished, of course, and also hunted deer, pheasant and other game whose home was the forest, including the bird called "chachalaca." And of course, Akumal being a coconut plantation, coconuts were plentiful..

Right after dropping anchor, the lovers were greeted by Akumalecos in their cayucos. Taj and Natasha then spent that day—and many more—with the Akumalecos. That first night was a feast: *t'kin 'xik*—fish spiced with *achiote* wrapped in banana leaves then baked in a pit. Afterwards, Taj danced in the sand with one arm swinging free to the wheezy strains of Natasha's harmonica.

It would be in Akumal that Natasha and Taj would enjoy their most idyllic existence.

They would read: Taj his gift from Natasha of J.R.R. Tolkien's *The Lord of the Rings,* and Natasha her gift from Taj of a book of poems by the medieval Sufi mystic Jalal al-Din Rumi plus her gift from Michael A. of Eric Fromm's *The Art of Loving.* Taj and Natasha would also listen to Radio Havana for news of the quest for democracy in Czechoslovakia being called "Prague Spring." Their music never left them, of course. Taj the percussionist would beach-comb daily for various-sized cocos which he would halve, hollow and turn into percussion instruments. Together he and Natasha, on harmonica, would serenade dolphins, sea turtles and birds, all of which seemed drawn to their music. Pelicans hovered, pheasants watched from the forest, a flamingo circled in flight, sandpipers and gulls gathered—even the parrots in the royal palms seemed to stop squawking out of respect. Some evenings by the sea, on the beach, beneath the stars and coconut palms there were jam sessions with Taj, Natasha and various Akumalecos using the jaw bones of wild pigs to coax uniquely exotic beats out of an overturned cayuco.

The lovers' days became simple rhythms. At first light Taj would stand on the bowsprit and greet the dawn with yoga while Natasha would raise herself up to the top of the main mast in a bosun's chair and sing the new songs she and Taj had composed. Then the lovers would have a breakfast of tropical fruits in the *Zak Be's* cockpit. Next they would gear up on the dive platform off the stern and plunge head first to dive the canyons laced with black coral beyond the reef. A light lunch would be followed by reading and siestas. After a seafood dinner their nights beneath the stars would be dedicated to making music and dancing with one arm swinging free.

· · ·

During one siesta in Akumal Natasha dreamt a dream full of feelings.

She lay in the Maya blue hamaca her lover had strung between the *Zak Be's* forestay and the main mast. Above her, for shade, Taj had strung a tarp between the forestay and the main. Taj had also

45

hung the dreamcatcher from the forestay. The dream that Natasha dreamt that siesta was a recurring dream, one she had been having ever since she had loosened the bond between herself and her father. In the dream she was hard at work at what, according to her father, she was born to do: stand beside him on a street corner. This particular corner was the southwest corner of the Drag and 23rd Street.

The year was 1953, first grade for most, but not for Natasha. Her father home-schooled Natasha so that every morning they could go down to the Drag and 23rd Street. There they would stand on the southwest corner and Natasha would sing "Jesus Wants Me for a Sunbeam" while her father preached the Word of God to the "heathens"—the University students passing by. Because Natasha dreamt in color it was easy for her to picture the little dress her father made her wear: her Shirley Temple dress. The dress was white with an empire waist that was embroidered with red, white and blue flowers. To Natasha it seemed she had to stand there forever in her too small Buster Brown shoes while singing to attract the heathens so her father could rail at them with the gospel. In the dream her father was always dressed in his rumpled white suit and work boots. His tie was black and his eyes were afire with brimstone as he delivered the Word of God from the tattered St. James Bible he kept open to Luke 11—the Lord's prayer.

And so the dream always went: she would be singing and her father would be preaching, the tone of the dream as relentless as her father's baritone drone until the dreaming Natasha would say to her subconscious "Enough is enough." She would then turn over and go back to sleep.

But after awakening from the dream in the hamaca beneath the tarp that one siesta in Akumal, Natasha said a silent "thank you" to the dreamcatcher above her. She felt relieved for she had decided that her recurring dream was not a bad dream, merely a peek at the past and it had freed her to get in touch with her feelings. It also pleased her after that siesta to see, off to the west, seven puffy white cumulus clouds marching single file across the baby blue sky.

It occurred to her that they looked like music notes.

This was when she began to wonder what it would be like to *see* music.

. . .

The bull snake that was allowed to live at Rancho Quien Sabe as long it did not make a pig of himself had come out to enjoy the evening. Right now Mr. Bullsnake was slaked out along the home place's foundation of railroad ties. Near dark Mr. Bullsnake would slither off to disappear in the desert plant life: candelilla, sotol, creosote and greasewood. Eventually, Mr. Bullsnake would slither inside the privy with its panoramic view of the natural wonder that was the Big Empty. As Ben Jack Gage put it:

"The bestest goldurned view from a privy in South Brewster County bar *none!*"

It was here and only here that Mr. Bullsnake made a pig of himself.

. . .

It was Saturday, June 29, and Michael A. had just set down the newspaper. He was shaking his head and saying "Tsk, tsk" after reading about a plane passenger who had mistakenly thought he was entering an airliner's john only to open the wrong door and plunge thirty thousand feet to his demise somewhere over Missouri. Michael A. then looked at his stack of *Playboys* and found himself recalling a door he had once opened and had been pleasantly surprised by what was on the other side. It happened in the fall of 1954, second grade, Casis Elementary. Uncle Tunoose was there, too. He was standing in for Michael A.'s father.

It was one of those days in which Life had thrown a punch at both uncle and nephew.

Uncle Tunoose had just signed off on his third divorce, the cause of such, he had determined, being that line from Aesop about how "familiarity breeds contempt." He had decided that women were "another stupid human trick and nothin' but misery and pain, misery and pain." Michael A., meanwhile, was bummed out, too. His class

47

assignment that day was to bring a parent who would tell the class about their job. But Ma had to work and Michael A.'s father was stationed in Korea, so Uncle Tunoose came along—which turned out to be a disaster because Uncle Tunoose stood up and told everybody that he was "a pool parlor dude, you know, a pool hustler." The teacher was flabbergasted, the class roared and Michael A. was humiliated.

That evening Michael A. was still bummed-out. With a Tootsie Roll stuck in the side of his mouth like a pool parlor dude's cigar, Michael A. had plopped down on the front porch steps and lost himself as only an only child can by opening the door to his imagination. Once beyond that door, Michael A. drew his favorite cartoon character on a page of his Big Chief tablet. This was when Uncle Tunoose dropped by to make amends. As a sop Uncle Tunoose gave his nephew one of the hottest selling toys of 1953, a Slinky. While Michael A. sent the Slinky slowly somersaulting down the front porch steps and was mesmerized by its slow motion progress via gravity and inertia, Uncle Tunoose took a gander at his nephew's Big Chief tablet and liked what he saw in Michael A.'s rendition of his favorite cartoon character, Marvin the Martian, an ant who wore a Roman centurion's skirt and helmet and whose head was nothing but a black sphere of darkness with no mouth, only large expressive eyes. Below the drawing Michael A. had written Marvin's trademark line "Where's the kaboom?"

"Impressive, nephew, very impressive," said Uncle Tunoose. "You may be a smart aleck kid what's always poppin' off but this shows me you got vision and imagination, both of which can be worthwhile in this life, even providential."

"I can do better," Michael A. said, chomping his Tootsie Roll like it was a Swisher Sweet cigar. "I wanta be expert at it."

Uncle Tunoose said, "So ya got a sense of purpose too, huh? Well, I like that and I wanta promote it." He then took out a wad of dollar bills from his trouser pocket and peeled off a few. Next, from his back pocket, he brought out the first ever edition of *Playboy* and handed both the money and magazine to Michael A. "You might find this rag inspirational—it's got some good cartoons. The dinero's for art materials."

Now, nearly sixteen years later, Saturday, June 29, in the dining room of the 19th Street house, during Saturday morning cartoons on the Stromberg Carlson television set, Marvin the Martian was again saying "Where's the kaboom?" And this caused Michael A. to open the door to his imagination again ... and—surprise, surprise—it turned out to be the door to opportunity.

He just hoped he was not about to step into a free fall like that poor guy somewhere over Missouri.

. . .

Michael A. was seated in the straight back chair at the head of the black church-door-turned-dining-room-table. In front of him was the 19th Street piggy bank—the three lock box that held the profits from Purple People Eater Productions' movie showings at Batts Auditorium and the Academic Center Auditorium. But Michael A. was not counting that money; no, he was counting what he had made so far from the eighty pounds of one-pound bricks of marijuana in Jen's two olive green Samsonite suitcases, the ones he had flown to Boston with that Saturday morning six weeks ago.

Before counting this money a second time, though, he read the letters in the box, the ones from France during World War I by a soldier named "Abe." The letters had been mailed to Miss Mona Devine, 200 West 19th Street, Austin, Texas and said Abe loved Mona and wanted to marry her after the war, take her away from 19th and University so they could start a new life together. It was the Department of the Army telegram in the box saying Abe had been killed in action that made Michael A. sneer and say:

"War—*hah!*—what's it good for? ... Nothin' but death and destruction."

Then, for the second time, Michael A. counted the pot profits. Again he placed the bills in $1000 stacks, a rubber band securing each stack. He arranged the money this way because Uncle Tunoose had told him that was the way it was done. Michael A. calculated that his profit was $5500. He figured this was about right, the pot having cost $4000 plus expenses—a round trip plane flight, a night in the downtown Hilton Hotel and a little something for Uncle Tunoose's bag man, Cool Breeze. After taking out another $6000 for Uncle Tunoose—all of it going to Uncle Tunoose's lawyer—it added up to $5500 for Michael A. The guy in Boston, the amiable oaf who called himself Mugsy, was due to make the other half of the payoff—another 16K—soon and that would mean another $7500 for Michael A.

$13,000 profit seemed like a sweet deal to Mister Hoochie Coochie Man.

Then Michael A. started wondering why he was eating all the expenses and Uncle Tunoose wasn't chipping in half.

But then Michael A. recalled something that Uncle Tunoose had once said: "In the life what I lead truth an' love are seldom-seen dividends."

So, feeling prosperous enough, Michael A. shined the notion of going halvsies on expenses with Uncle Tunoose. He had decided he would write off the expense under the heading of "Respect."

Michael A. was next reminded how much he missed his band. Not only did those guys keep him grounded, they gave him life through truth and love and companionship. So, feeling prosperous and a little grateful, Michael A. counted out a sufficient amount of funds for seven season passes to Barton Springs. Then Michael A. thought a while longer and, feeling even more prosperous and a lot more generous, put all the $5500 in the three lock box and said:

"House Rule Number One: 'If you're not there, you don't get any' is hereby suspended due to lack of a quorum."

After that, for the first time since his army misadventure, he took his burgundy Triumph 650 motorcycle out for a spin—what those in his peer group called "cruising for burgers."

· · ·

Uncle Tunoose often said, "The first thing you learn in this life is that you got to wait."

50

But waiting had always been tough on Michael A.

Save for his mustard-con-ketchup-stained army green boxer shorts, his body was bare. Having finished off his two Mooreburgers-con-extra-cheese-extra-fries, he pushed his chair away from the dining room table. His blurry eyes fixed on William Bendix playing the title role in *The Life of Riley*. For some reason seeing ol' Rile below Thelma Lou and Barney's goldfish bowl atop the Stromberg Carlson television set in the floor-to-ceiling bookcase inspired Michael A to quote the tag lines of TV comics and personalities:

"'Annnd how sweet it is'—Jackie Gleason."

"'Thanks for the memories'—Bob Hope."

"'Really good show'—Ed Sullivan."

"'I dood it!'—Red Skelton."

"'Wwwelll!'—Jack Benny."

Then Michael A. stood up and, reeling a bit, said, "Down to seeds and stems again an' that means I got to raid the Hotpoint." Next, to William Bendix, he said, "An' what a revolting development we do indeed have here, Rile. Ol' Flaws'n Foibles, the sole surviving son, returns from Boot Camp Hell to find himself home alone. Ain't *nooo*body here. No Natasha, no Taj, no Jack and Jen, no Nacho, no Uncle Tunoose to tell me I got to wait—not even those sorry fleabag goshdurned dogs Wiley'n Beep Beep . . . and that stinkin' Cool Breeze won't set foot in here on accounta the *haint*."

Next, as Katie Winters came on the Stromberg Carlson to sell Michael A. some Ice Blue Secret deodorant, he picked up his third—or maybe fourth—quart of Old Milwaukee. After opening it with the church key and taking a deep pull on it, he again remembered that he was down to seeds and stems so he headed for the kitchen. But as Michael A. padded into the darkened kitchen on bare feet he paused at the sounds of itty bitty feet scurrying in all directions. After a clumsy slap at the light switch and as Mr. Whipple on the Stromberg Carlson failed again to keep his hands off the Charmin, the kitchen came alive . . .

. . . and Michael A. nearly jumped out of his skin.

"Leapin' lizards, I've soiled the nest again," he said, eyes full of fear and awe at what he saw. "If Jen comes back'n sees all these roaches, she'll have me hamstrung."

Now for the first time he also smelled the garbage and saw the dust motes and waxy yellow buildup in the kitchen.

It was a sensory awakening that made Michael A. realize it was time to do the right thing: he would move Ma into the 19th Street house.

. . .

It was afternoon. Living with Ma was as it had always been: she resided in her world and Michael A. in his. For the umpteenth time he was hearing Ma's old RCA Victrola playing "Stardust" by Austin's very own Little Jimmy Valentine. But Ma—bless her heart— had gotten rid of those dust motes. No smell of garbage and there was no debris–littered interior, either. Ma had even spit-polished the Hotpoint refrigerator, the Tappan electric range, the nearly new Waring blender and equally nearly new Sunbeam toaster.

However, as Michael A. well knew, Ma was not going to cook— she never had because she was afraid of fire. Ma did surprise Michael A. with all her activities, though. The church ladies corralled her for bake sales and bingo nights. They took her to Wonderful Wednesday at Scholz's Beer Garten. There was Thursday night wrestling at Palmer Municipal Auditorium. There was "Girls Night Out" at the Night Hawk Restaurant.

Ma was one busy old biddy.

So Michael A. still had a lot "Me Time" and consequently it seemed as if he were saying "Down to seeds and stems again" a lot.

And every night Mona the Haint was there somewhere.

Now, with Ma all moved in and watching *As the World Turns* on her big Philco TV down in his old bedroom. Michael A. was upstairs with the Stromberg Carlson on and saying to himself, "Yeah, okay, family first, moving Ma in is a compromise . . . an' life is compromise." But then he grimaced mightily and slammed the quart of Old Milwaukee down hard on the church-door-turned-dining-room-table. Next, as the beer spurted out, spilled onto his army green boxer shorts, in as miserable a voice as he'd ever before mustered—sincerely, anyway—his eyes bugged out and he said:

"Oh god, oh god, oh god, it's come to this—and this has gotta be the epitome of absurd juxtaposition."

For right now on the Stromberg Carlson was *To Tell The Truth* moderator Bud Collier and the sight of Bud in his smarmy bow tie was too much for Michael A., who was now pounding his fist on the table and saying in a low drone:

"Game shows. I've sunk to a new all-time low—I'm watching afternoon *game* shows. *To Tell the Truth, Concentration, The Match Game,* Bud Collier, Peggy Cass, Kitty Carlisle, Gene Raymond ... oh god, oh god, oh god—what's next? I might as well be dead meat on a stick."

It was then that he lifted his head, eyes tearing up and searching woefully, his lower lip trembling as he said in a pleading, desperate scream at the top of his lungs:

"Maaa! What's next?"

"*The Edge of Night,*" said a voice from downstairs. "It's on Channel 7."

What was *really* weird, though, was that it did not sound like Ma.

. . .

Cool Breeze—now sporting a star lily in his afro courtesy of Connelly's Florist— was on the west side of the house weeding the garden when he saw Michael A. walking up. Pausing to lean on his hoe, Cool Breeze said:

"Well, if it ain't Mister-Hoochie-Coochie-Man-what-was-da-Man-from-Uncle-Sam an' what is once again da Man from Uncle Tunoose." Then Cool Breeze managed to lean on his hoe even more and say, "'Tis an unweeded garden that grows to seed.'"

"Yeah, yeah," Michael said, "an' 'Things rank and gross in Nature possess it merely.'" Then, tone upbeat, he said, "Guess what? I found a mannequin in the garage that somebody dressed up like a leprechaun."

"Yeah, that's a leftover from the Gamma Sigs' St. Patrick Day bash."

"How 'bout if I made a Marvin the Martian scarecrow to ward off the grackles?"

"I got an old broom you can use to make Marvin stand up straight'n scary."

"Got any rope or twine?"

"Use the vines on that there chimney."

When Michael A. looked over at the vines, he saw that they were climbing a red brick chimney up to the roof of the 19th Street house. Scratching his head, he said, "I had no idea a chimney was there."

"There's a lot you don't know is here," Cool Breeze said, and walked away.

An hour later Michael A. had assembled his Marvin the Martian scarecrow. "All it lacks," he told Cool Breeze when he brought it out to the garden, "is his green centurion helmet."

"Gotcha covered," Cool Breeze said and handed Michael A. an army helmet he had painted Martian green and mounted an old push brush. "Recycle this too," he said. "It belonged to another centurion in a faraway land."

Michael A. grinned and said, "Where was the kaboom?"

"Was in Vietnam," Cool Breeze said solemnly.

Cool Breeze then picked up a nearby Connelly's Florist bucket and began to spread rotting flowers as moisture bearers for the beans, tomatoes, squash and chiles growing in the shade of at the corn plants. It was when Michael A. was placing Marvin in the garden that he saw that, under the thin coat of green paint, the name "Brown" had originally been stenciled on the helmet.

As in: Jackson Lamar Brown aka "Cool Breeze."

. . .

Michael A. was bored and lonely, so he resolved to get out more. It had become obvious to him that what was a building block in his Reality—The Fine Art of Hanging Out in the '60s—was not sustaining him.

"Way, wayyy too much Me Time," he would all too often hear himself muttering. "Too much Old Milwaukee, too much down to seeds and stems again."

So this morning Michael A. rose from the faded red couch in the living room to run through the dining room and kitchen then out the back door and down its steps into the backyard. At the 1956 pink Cadillac he yelled through its back passenger window:

"Haint alert!"

Cool Breeze's sleepy response was that he had no time to cruise for burgers as he had to mow the lawn, weed and water the garden as well as tend to his "recyclin' bizmesses."

So Michael A. ambled on past the garage and Cool Breeze's "recyclables": piles of brown, green and clear bottles, empty food and beer cans. Next he headed north on the sidewalk. Once on campus he paused at the Tower's main entrance to read its sixty-foot long inscription above that entrance: "Ye Shall Know the Truth and the Truth Shall Make You Free." Next he meandered over to the West Mall to listen to whoever was opining from atop the oak stump there. Ryder and Bicycle Annie were there, each with a burlap bag they had just filled with recyclables for Cool Breeze. Just as Dick Reavis was all set to mount the stump Bicycle Annie beat him to it. Before a gathering of maybe fifty-odd folks she opined on a 1968 current event: the implementation of the nation's new health care bill, Medicare. Annie called it Greed-i-care and summed it up this way:

"Mark my words, ladies and gents, future historians will declare Greed-i-care a seed of destruction for us fellow Americans. Greed-i-care is a blank check for doctors, insurance companies, their lawyers—*all* of those who live off the ills of others. Greed-i-care will allow them to gouge the price for health, life, even death. These parasites will prosper at the expense of others due to their being so self involved, so bent on self magnification . . . and therefore they will be one of the causes for why this country shall ultimately collapse under its own weight."

The smart aleck in Michael A. then popped by saying, "Right on, Annie, tell it like it is."

Whereupon Annie summed Michael A. up, too, by pointing at him and saying, "Well, if it ain't the unweeded garden what's goin' ta seed. Ohhh, yesss"—practically hissing—"for twas the summer of 1968 at the 19th Street house when *two* went west, *two* flew south *annnd* this 'un here got hisself lost in the nest."

Freaky as that was, Michael A. kept his cool and flashed her the peace sign before taking his leave by affecting an imitation of a Furry Freak Brother's long, exaggerated strides. He took the short walk to the Student Union and then into the Chuck Wagon—but not take his regular table for it had been taken over by Philistines claiming to be Classics majors, Philosophy majors, Fine Arts majors. So Michael A. took another table to nurse his half pint of Superior Dairies Homogenized Milk, eat his twenty-cent bowl of peaches and peruse the *Daily Texan*. To anyone passing by who gave him even a glimpse, he said:

"Have you heard that new word in the American lexicon—body count?" Then: "See me? I'm drowning in sublime *loon*liness."

And that was how Michael A.'s mornings now went. His afternoons were spent trying to beat the heat, mainly by riding around town on his Triumph 650—"cruising for burgers." He visited naturally cool spots such as Barton Springs, Hamilton Pool, Campbell's Hole, Deep Eddy, Lake Austin and that hollow on Lake Travis where folks skinnydipped. He even went to the grotto in the bend on Waller Creek behind Helen M. Kirby Hall to work on his music. For lunch he frequented air-conditioned burger joints: both Holiday Houses, 2-Js, The Stallion, Sandy's, Hut's, The Toddle House, Whataburger, Kirschner's, Dirty Martin's, Hank's, GM Steakhouse plus that new place at Capital Plaza that claimed to have served up more than a million burgers, McDonald's.

By late afternoon he was in the cool dark air-conditioned environs of the local movie houses such as The Americana, Paramount, State, Capital Plaza. He watched *Bullit* so many times he knew all of Steve McQueen's lines.

56

At home Michael A. tried to make a comfort zone of his immediate and constant surroundings. He tacked up his Marlon Brando, James Dean and Che Guevara posters beside the American flag on the living room wall. He kept his almost new Judy Jetson lunch box and lava lamp alongside his stack of *Playboys*, the newest *Playboy* open to a Vargas or Gahan Wilson cartoon. He also let the five kittens—the white one Hannah and the four calicos, Hazel, Dot, Persia and Phoebe—roam the house but, mostly what they did was collectively snooze—and shed cat hair—on the faded red couch in the living room.

But being alone in the house became too creepy because Michael A. became convinced that Miss Mona Devine was intent on driving him to madness. He believed that to lie all by himself on that faded red couch in the living room of the 19th Street, to lie there in the dark while the shadows were running from themselves down in the White Room—to do so was to court Devine madness. Michael A. heard sounds—a door closing downstairs, a creak, a groan—yet no source could be found. He heard whispers that could not have been the wind ... and those nearby scratching sounds were almost never from a kitten wanting outside. He had feelings of abandonment. He missed his housemates. Especially Natasha. Boy oh boy did he miss Natasha. And Daphne? Man, that nut-job-former-girlfriend wanted no part of him. When he had called her up to see if she would do her patriotic duty by welcoming home the returning veteran with open arms, she had said:

"Dry up and blow away, Michael A. You were only in the army for two measly weeks."

"But"—putting some whine his tone—"I was out there in Harm's Way, caught up in the Big Wind, fending off the Cold Cruel World's fangs with just my wits."

"Grow up, Michael A., quit languishing in self loathing—and *stop* pestering me."

"Mubblefubble. Women are nothin' but misery an' pain, misery'n pain.

Maybe worst of all, though, Michael A. felt that he was becoming what his father had predicted: a slug, a sloth, a couch-slacker—one of nature's layabouts. Except that he was not trying to skate through life as much as he was stuck in the mud. Not only was he losing his perspective, he was straying from Oscar Wilde's dictum of "the main aim is to amuse yourself."

He was also feeling the xutan of his twenty-first birthday, which he most definitely did not want to spend alone.

Or with Ma.

Or Mona.

Just like Bicycle Annie had said: he was lost in the nest.

Chapter Five

Jen was seated on Rancho Quien Sabe's front porch stoop with
Wiley and Beep Beep lying down in front of her. Jen was having to
lean forward so that she could doctor Beep Beep's paw for toritos
and diablitos. In between plucking out these stickers Jen was looking woefully over at Wiley whose right jowl was swollen twice its
size from a snake bite. Fortunately, both dogs were distracted by
a nearby woodpecker as it pecked away at a tree-like cactus Jack
called a *cholla*. Jen did not look up when Jack pulled up in the Fitty
Six and thumped his left hand on the outside of the truck's door to
announce his arrival.

"We got mail," he said.

"Where"—plucking a torito sticker from Beep Beep's paw—"do
we get mail?"

"It gets dropped off at Current Events," Jack said as he got out
of the Fitty Six holding a package.

"That river rafting place over in Salsipuedes?"

Jack did not answer. By now he was on the porch and Wiley and
Beep Beep were watching him intently. "This mail's from Mexico,"
he said. "It's from Natasha an' Taj an' Nacho." Tearing off the
package's pink paper revealed a jar of honey and two pair of Maya
chanclas—open-toed sandals with thick black rubber soles made of
used tire treads with *sisal* rope attached to the soles to secure one's
feet. Handing Jen the smaller pair of chanclas, he said, "In Yucatan

59

they take old tire tread an' sisal rope an' make chanclas. 'Waste not want not' is la maya way."

"Recycling," Jen said.

"Say *whut*?"

"Recycling. Like what Cool Breeze does. 'Recycling' is the politically correct way of saying 'waste not want not.'"

"Lawsy mercy,"— frowning now—"why do folks have to come up with newfangled ways of sayin' old-fashioned ideas?" Then, frowning some more he said, "Jennn?"

"Yes?"

"What's that mean anyway—'politically correct'?"

. . .

Jack and Jen had just finished their part of a community chore: making wax. Since there was no electricity hereabouts, everybody used candles. So some river folk gathered candelilla, some hauled the candelilla to the vat needed to process it and Jack and Jen's part of the effort was to make the wax. Later, they would take it to the candle factory in Alpine.

"Hon," Jack said, "you look all tuckered out."

Jen said nothing, just let the large, flat rock she was lying on cool her body while she was submerged an inch below the Rio Grande and in the shade of the Mexican side of Santa Elena Canyon. It helped that Wiley and Beep Beep were frolicking nearby and refreshing the exposed part of her parched body with cascades of river water.

Unlike Jen, Jack seemed happy as a clam. In fact, he had been downright cheerful all day long, even when he had declared the temperature to be "112 in the shade." Since before sunup he had been chirping like a songbird, a smile in his voice as he prodded Jen out of their hamaca while she was still washing the sleep from her eyes. He gave her coffee and oatmeal made on their rusty mesquite-fired wood stove. Then he had insisted that she put on Granma Gage's boots, a longsleeved khaki shirt and sunbonnet.

What really got Jen, however, was that Jack had done the dishes. Ben Jack Gage was a new man now that he was back in Far West

Texas "down along the Rio Grande." Gone was the surly over-heat-ed sourpuss about to flunk out of school right into the draft. There was no sign of the nocturnal creature who played his guitar all night long in the White Room, either; though music still stirred within him, especially when he and Jen finessed some kickass double leads on their guitars during their evenings at Rancho Quien Sabe.

Right now, however, on that large, partially submerged flat rock in the Rio Grande, Jen was raising her head up just enough to peer through her tired eyelids and see Jack knee deep in the metal vat set in the river bank sand as he stomped candelilla into the first stage of making wax. Today's first chore—after paddling *Analuz* up river into the great maw that was the mouth of Santa Elena Canyon—had been to haul buckets of water. Jack took two buckets at a time and Jen took one the fifty feet up from the river to the wax vat. Once the buried-in-the-sand vat was full, they began pulling candelilla plants from sixty-pound bundles stacked taller than Jen, maybe fifty bundles in all.

Hauling water and then setting mounds of candelilla took up the morning thereby taking away the shade from the United States side of the canyon. So while the shade shifted to the Mexican side of Santa Elena Jack and Jen played guitars in between having a lunch of flour tortillas and beans with onions and jalapenos. Jack and Jen had then climbed into the vat and tromped each and every candelilla plant down below the water, steadily tromping until no plant was above the surface. Once all the candelilla was stomped to Jack's approval, a fitted piece of plywood was dropped over the vat. The plywood had a hole cut in its middle wide enough to fit a piece of tin flashing down and around the hole's perimeter. After they had scooped out the hole, Jack lit a fire in the hole and once the water was stirred to a boil, sulfuric acid was added. Once the wax started floating to the surface—looking much like the oatmeal Jack had made for breakfast—Jack used a six-inch wide, blacksmith-fashioned metal skimmer with a long handle to scoop the wax into two fifty-five gallon drums. When each load of candelilla became wax it had to dry before it could be placed in burlap bags.

"Jaaack?" Jen said while holding her eyes shut in the coolness of the submerged rock.

"Yeah, hon." Voice still happy as a clam.

"Tell me again why we did all this hard labor, why we worked like dogs."

"Well, first off, dogs don't work a lick, Jen. 'Specially them two what's ours—when'd ya ever see either of 'em do anything but eat, poop, bark an' play?"

"Doesn't matter. They love us."

"They durn well better."

"But tell me again why we're doing the candelilla."

"You could say that it's a rite of passage."

Jen's dead-tired sapphire eyes were on a dragon fly circling above her as she said, "Did you know that 'sincere' comes from the Latin words *sin cerus*?"

"You gettin' delirious on me, Jen?"

"Nooo. 'Sin cerus' means 'without wax.' It was how the Romans described their best marble columns. You see, most of their columns had to be waxed so as to fill the fissures in them."

Chuckling now, Jack said, "So 'sincere' means 'phony finish'."

This was when Wiley and Beep Beep began keening, the eyes of each fixed on the top of Santa Elena Canyon's Mexican side. Placing his left hand against his forehead Indian style, Jack looked up there and said:

"I make out an even dozen."

"Los Boys?"

"It's them all right."

. . .

They drove to Alpine with the burlap bags of dried candelilla wax in the bed of the Fitty Six. There they went to the candle factory on West Highway 90 and cut a deal for their order of candles. Next they went to C.G. Morrison Hardware and bought a Motorola transistor radio and a supply of batteries. That night, before picking up their guitars, they sat on the front porch and listened to

Wolfman Jack. The first song he played was "Winchester Cathedral" by the New Vaudeville Band.

"A body's got to have music, right, Jen?" Bobbing his head in time to the music.

"A body sure enough does," she said while keeping the beat with a Nocona.

. . .

Though it was *atardecer*—dusk—Jack again said he bet it was 112 in the shade and Jen again believed it but was sure that it was more comfortable than Austin.

Jack and Jen—and the other fifty-five gallon drum of candelilla—were going up the Rio Bravo in *Analuz* thanks to a small outboard motor. At the great maw that was the mouth of Santa Elena Canyon they saw a little black bear sunning itself on a rock.

"That bear's a guardian of the Otherworld," Jack said. Then paused and said, "I wonder if that little guy might be my *uay*." Saying it "way."

"What's a 'uay'?"

"It's a Maya thing," Jack said. "La maya believe that everybody has a uay—usually a soul companion from the world of nature."

"Then maybe that's myyy uay up there," Jen said, pointing up at a peregrine falcon perched atop a now-purple pinnacle on the Mexican side's wall of the great maw.

"The mate is over there," Jack said, pointing at another peregrine atop the United States side of Santa Elena's thousand-foot-high wall.

Jen said, "I wonder if they're like us and building a nest nearby."

"The peregrine's the fastest bird in the world," Jack said. "They say it can dive at almost two-hundred miles an hour."

Getting a dreamy look, Jen said, "Maybe they've already built their nest and they've got a clutch of eggs in it. Or maybe that clutch has hatched and they've got babies to feed."

"Been known to happen, hon, been known to happen."

. . .

Jack said that, as in Palenque, they were on the cusp of "legendary time."

Jack was saying this because on this night Venus and Jupiter were paired in the eastern sky.

By nightfall the lovers had arrived, like Palenque, at yet another ancient crossroads: the intersection of Fern Canyon and Santa Elena Canyon. Here they dragged *Analuz* onto the Mexican shore and offloaded a barrel of candelilla. Jack kindled a fire next and then they waited. They passed the time dining on tumbleweeds and tortillas while peering up through the narrow window to heaven formed by Santa Elena's 1200-foot walls. As the sky seemed to pass over their heavenly window, Jack pointed out the Zodiac constellations as well as a necklace of Maya constellations. Among the countless points of light were shooting stars, the waning moon and a moving point of light Jack said was a new intruder in 1968's sky.

A satellite.

. . .

Late that evening a voice called out from above the canyon.

"*Bis be'.*" Saying it "bees BAYYY."

"*Bis be',*" Jack said, calling back. Then to Jen he said, "It's Los Boys."

Soon Nacho showed up riding a burro. Though he appeared happy to see them, the old daykeeper took a long look around before signaling "okay" to Los Boys by making a run of notes on his wooden flute. Soon from the upper reaches of the Sierra del Carmen came burro after burro down the trail into Fern Canyon. Each of these little beasts of burden was loaded down with various smuggled goods in bundles and driven by Los Boys—*contrabandistas*. But these smugglers were not in fact just "los boys" but whole families of men, women and children. Jack told Jen that two of the bundles—*costales*—contained *mota* for Michael A. and that after leaving the Big Bend Nacho had traveled to Acapulco where he bought the mota from rebels then contracted Los Boys to deliver it here.

64

"Michael A's getting fifty kilos," Jack said to Jen, showing her a handful. "It aggravates Cuz to convert from kilos to pounds. He don't like moving mota on burros neither 'cause some turns into 'shake'."

"It's the color of gold dust," Jen said, and from behind her heard Nacho say:

"So let us call it 'Acapulco Gold'."

· · ·

It marveled Jen to hear her man speak Spanish with Los Boys. It also marveled her to watch the smugglers move with precise grace in their time-honored trade. In less than an hour Los Boys had unloaded the contraband from the burros onto three wooden rafts that had come out of nowhere to this ancient crossroads of canyons. As the bundles passed from hand to hand down the trail to the river and onto the wooden rafts, Jen saw it symbolically: sands of time moving through the hour glass.

"It's called "drifting wood," she heard Jack say beside her. "For centuries smugglers have been transporting their goods via raft on the Rio Bravo. I've known some of Los Boys all my life. Drifting wood is part of their family's way of making a living. Being illegal don't make it wrong, Jen."

"It's dangerous," she said.

Later, what Nacho called a "pagan *pachanga*" ensued: the case of Senor Fuego bought from Aguilar's was broken open and its bottles passed around a campfire crowded with guitars playing and voices singing. Jen and the other women and children danced barefoot in the sand with one arm swinging free. Jen was thrilled to see her campfire shadow cast ten-feet tall on one of Fern Canyon's red-flickering walls. When a deep blue darkness moved in over the canyon followed by an *aguacero*—a shower—Jack held a rain slicker over Jen. Again she was thrilled, this time to know that this rare rain would wash grains of sand into the river and, like tiny dancers, give themselves up to its ever onward flow to the sea. She was thrilled yet again to peer skyward and make out a white starlit cloud within the small squall. "White rain" Jack said to her, and white rain it was: hard and bullet-like as it pelted Fern Canyon. Once the aguacero passed, its progeny—a trickle of rainwater—made its entry from above and down the canyon's south wall to grow into a two-foot wide waterfall. This thin veil of Mother Nature's mist so enthralled Jen that she fell under its spell, was drawn over to and within it. There she closed her eyes and let the cascade wash her clean, cleaner than ever before. She was daydreaming about dinosaurs once being here to bathe and get a drink of water when she sensed her lover's presence. Feeling his strength beside her, Jen's eyes opened to find Jack now part of the waterfall, too. Now their naked flesh was within falling shimmering rainbows and making the sound of a private downpour. Being by now in their relationship oh-so-comfortable within their bodies, the lovers bridged the few inches between them and made themselves into one big hug. As Jen raised up on her tiptoes and placed her mouth to Jack's left ear, she said:

"I am another like yourself."

"And I am you and you are me and we are us."

· · ·

Jack and Jen found Nacho atop a boulder. He was perched on his haunches like a Maya leprechaun and holding his wooden flute to his lips so as to allow the flute to conjure a lilting tune. Drawn to his presence same as she had been drawn to the waterfall, Jen went to him, this wizened old soul with a gleam in his eyes. To her, his aura there in the delicate shadow of Fern Canyon was like the rainbows within the waterfall: it shimmered—but not with colors, just silver shimmers of lightning that produced a ballet of tiny dancers undulating to the rhythm of his flute's lilting tune.

Jen said, "Not only are you the bee who pollinates the flowers, you are dancing lightning."

Nacho's dark eyes brightened and he took the flute from his lips and said, "Yesss, I ammm Dancing Lightning. That is precisely what my uay would say too." Then, twinkling those wise old eyes: "And you are Walks in Beauty and he"—pointing at Jack—"is Like

66

the Night." Giggling now, he rose and, there atop the rock, waving one arm free, he danced for her, danced the Dance of the Jaguar Warrior.

Later that night, as another elf owl hooted its call from somewhere above, love was spoken with the Language of Touch all around that smoldering campfire. Fern Canyon became a crossroads on yet another level. Something had happened when Jen heard Jack speak Spanish with the smugglers. She had always known that Jack spoke Spanish but it had not occurred to her how different he spoke it than English. Gone was the Texan in his tone, replaced by a mild eloquence that enunciated and pronounced every syllable as clearly and as sharply as a rider gentling a horse with soft yet potent sounds. . . and it turned her on.

. . .

In each and every phone call lately Uncle Tunoose had said, "The first thing ya learn is ya got to wait."

And every day since Ma had moved in she had said, "She is Tiny Dancer, she is Rain Shadow, she is White Rain. Mona just likes you is all—nothing else to it."

It was Sunday night, June 30, and from somewhere within the house Mona was making a screeching, unnerving noise like fingernails raking across a chalkboard. So Michael A. had bugged out from the faded red couch. He decided to shave first then squeeze some zits, he went through Natasha's bedroom and into the upstairs bathroom that Natasha shared with Taj. Michael A. of course peeked in on the scene of the crime, Taj's bedroom. It was still minimalist to the max. Next Michael A. lathered up his face with Aerosol then stuck his chin out and was putting the Wilkinson Sword Blade to his throat when he froze with fear. He could not believe what he saw in the mirror: his face looked like he had been in a fight with a rosebush. Instinctively grabbing the crotch of his army green boxer shorts, he said:

"Heavens to mercatroids, good grief an' leapin' lizards—I'm not only being scared witless, I'm being carved up."

67

"Nooo, you aren't, silly boy," said a female voice from somewhere within the walls. "You passed out face first in the pizza again."

. . .

It was 5:30 P.M., Monday, July 1, and on the CBS Evening Blues Uncle Walter was broadcasting from The Vast Wasteland that a DC-3 with fifteen passengers on aboard had been hijacked to Cuba. But Michael A. missed it because he was out on the front porch in a purple butterfly chair reading Austin's underground newspaper *The Rag*.

. . .

On Tuesday, July 2, it happened again and this time Michael A. was there to learn all about it.

He was in his army green boxer shorts and seated at the black church-door-turned-dining-room-table. He was on a massive fooder: sucking down a jumbo Dr. Pepper while devouring a Mooreburger and large fries, extra ketchup. He was watching Uncle Walter on the CBS Evening Blues and from within their fish bowl above the Stromberg Carlson television set in the floor-to-ceiling bookcase, Thelma and Barney Lou were watching Michael A.'s every slurpin'-munchin' move.

"I already fed you guys," he said to Thelma and Barney. "Like my old man used to say every time he brought burgers home, 'I always take care of my dependents.'" Then Michael A. wolfed down a big hunk of Mooreburger—only to freeze mid swallow as he heard Uncle Walter report that one Velasquez Fonseca, a Cuban, had hijacked a Boeing 727 jet airliner with 92 passengers aboard and commandeered it to Cuba. Michael A.'s reaction, after swallowing and clearing his throat with a big gulp of Dr. Pepper, was to bang the black church-door-turned-dining-room-table with his free left fist then thrust up his arm and extend it in a power salute and say with firm conviction:

"*Cool* move, Velasquez! Martyrdom is the most sincere form of self destruction."

. . .

On Wednesday, July 3, it was disclosed by Uncle Walter on the CBS Evening Blues that the airline industry was briefing pilots on how to land at Havana's airport.

Michael A., however, was downing 39-cent quarts of Old Milwaukee. Hours later, at just after midnight, as the last television station—San Antonio's Channel 12—signed off with a shot of Old Glory flowing proudly in the breeze while playing the national anthem. So Michael A. pushed himself to a standing position and began to stagger away from the dining room table on wobbly legs. He came to a stop at the entrance to the kitchen and turned to look back through bloodshot eyes at the Stromberg Carlson television set. There he imagined in his alcoholic stupor that he saw fitness guru Jack Lalanne and his big white dog Happy exhorting an unseen audience to exercise.

"I know where the kaboom is, old man," he said to the imaginary Lalanne.

It was then that Ma appeared in the dining room, Hannah and the other four calico cats—Hazel, Dot, Persia and Phoebe—trailing her as if she were the Pied Piper. As Ma placed both hands on her hips a la Jen, Michael A. saw a Tarot deck in her apron pocket. Next she shook her head at her son and said in the *old* Ma's voice, the one full of fire and brimstone, the one she had used when raising her only child by herself:

"So this is what comes of folks with too much time on their hands. Perhaps as your father used to say you *are* a slacker, one of nature's layabouts who just wants to skate through life."

Michael A. grinned. He was glad to see that Ma was her old self again.

. . .

It was after nine o'clock on Wednesday evening, July 3, and Dylan's "Sad-eyed Lady of the Lowlands" was droning on. Michael A. was sprawled listlessly on the faded red couch in the living room. The Fine Art of Hanging Out had utterly collapsed. He had decided

69

that indeed he was a slacker, one of nature's layabouts, because he was two days behind in current events: the unread *Austin American-Statesman's* Sunday edition was spread out in a discarded fashion all over the hardwood floor amidst his portable library of *The Kama Sutra*, Ken Kesey's *One Flew Over the Cuckoo's Nest* and Joseph Heller's *Catch 22*. Michael A.'s going away gift to Natasha of Eric Fromm's *The Art of Loving* had been replaced by Richard Farina's *Been Down So Long It Looks Like Up To Me*. His stack of *Playboys* was still alongside his nearby Judy Jetson lunch box and lava lamp and at his feet was the first issue of *Rolling Stone Magazine*, the one with John Lennon on the cover. Draped over Michael A.'s face was this Sunday's *Parade Magazine* insert—but he did not know where his army green boxers were, so he was wearing nothing but a pair of white athletic socks and a T-shirt his father had brought him from Saigon. This particular T-shirt showed a baby on its back, the baby's tiny feet sticking up in air, both of the child's little hands wrapped around a baby bottle, the child nursing on the bottle's rubber nipple. Below this image the caption read:

People suck from the very beginning

Michael A. was thinking he was either going to nod off into oblivion beneath the *Parade Magazine* or else he was going to have to roll over and search around for the new *Furry Freak Brothers* comic he believed was beneath the faded red couch. Or—and this was pretty much out of the question—he would have to get up from the faded red couch and change the Dylan record on the Monkey Ward's Airline Stereo. Briefly, he cursed Taj—not because of Natasha, but because Taj had not finished his invention of a built-in gadget to make a turntable shut off automatically. Next Michael A. wished he could do what Barbara Eden's character on *I Dream of Jeanie* did: fold his arms across his chest, blink his eyes with a bob of his chin and *Shazam!*—the new Thirteenth Floor Elevators album "Easter Everywhere" would drop down onto the turntable, the record needle would fall in place and out would come Tommy Hall's jug jiving with Roky's Erickson's ethereal voice while

Stacy Sutherland's lead guitar did its wizardry, John Ike Walton and Benny Thurman holding up the bottom via drums and bass. Next Michael A.'s jambled mind began to ponder going back to school—only to decide right away that an impish stinker like him had too much of a commercial mind for such a commitment. He then considered getting a job because these days an able-bodied U.S. Army vet like him was a commodity in the World of Work Waltz. He was sure there was plenty of call for his kind.

But what he really wanted to do was shoot lightning through the sky.

Chapter Six

It was the United States of America's birthday.

Early that morning of Thursday, July 4, Jack had eyes only for Jen. He loved seeing her fine long legs below her short-shorts right down to her new chanclas. Her white peasant blouse hung just enough off her left shoulder for cleavage and her hair was atop her head beneath a white Yucatecan straw hat. Jack had on a cowboy hat, his best Levis, a long sleeve khaki shirt and Granpa Gage's Lucchese boots. Right now he and Jen were in the Fitty Six on the eighty-mile drive to Alpine for the annual Fourth of July parade. Even though they saw fewer than half a dozen vehicles on Highway 118, Jack gave the hidey-sign to each and every one.

In Alpine the parade watchers lined Holland Avenue like the town's divided housing: Latinos on the south side, Anglos on the north. Jack and Jen stood on the south side in the shade of the lumber yard. The parade watchers waved miniature American flags as they stood straight and proud. Each held a hand over their heart when the Alpine High School band marched by playing the national anthem and "America the Beautiful" and all felt the bass drum's patriotic beat in their heart.

Afterward they slurped down plain ol' vanilla shakes at the Dairy Dream Drive In.

. . .

It was late in the evening on Thursday, July 4. The *Austin American Statesman's* headline took up the entire front page but, because the newspaper was beneath a Shakey's pizza box on the black church-door-turned-dining-room-table, all that could be read was "Happy Flag-waving Fourth to Us All." So, after a throaty belch, Michael A. pushed aside the Shakey's Pizza box until it fell off the table and onto the floor. Michael A. now took a long pull on his quart of Old Milwaukee then set down the brown bottle and stood up. After steadying himself he marched into the kitchen along a litter trail of empty quarts of Old Milwaukee, crumpled up wax paper hamburger wrappers, empty half pints of Superior Dairies Homogenized Milk, peach pits, orange and apple and banana peels, grape stems, crumpled up paper towels, grease spots that seemed to be giving birth to waxy yellow buildup and a dead cockroach the size of a mouse. Entering the kitchen, he switched on the light and a phalanx of roaches fled before him. Wincing, he said:

"Ratz. Ma got the dust motes but missed the infestation—it's what I get for not having rinsed the beer bottles."

Now the *Furry Freak Brothers'* endless war with an army of cockroaches led by General Cucaracha came to mind and Marvin the Martian took over. Saying "Where's the kaboom? Where oh where is the kaboom?" Michael A. as Marvin went into the kitchen pantry there to peruse it until he found a can of Raid.

"Ah, *here's* the kaboom," he said, grabbing the Raid. He then storm-troopered around the kitchen using the can of Raid can as his terrible swift sword.

The body count was 1118 casualties.

Michael A. finished by collecting every empty, infestuous beer bottle and flinging them out the back door, their breakage waking Cool Breeze in the back seat of his pink 1956 Cadillac.

"*Hey!* What you think you doin' there, man?"

"Recyclin!"

. . .

Since the beginning of July there had been no shortage of "against the wind" days. Times when the appearance of dust devils—remolinos—in the distance was the progenitor of tumbleweeds dancing from west to east across the Chihuahua Desert, when all of Mother Nature dined on dust. Such days had Jen thinking back to Christmas break, 1967, when she and Jack were on Lake Austin in *Analuz* and were being washed clean by an early morning rain. It was in that moment that Jen had been leaning backwards on Jack's chest, his chin resting atop her head when he took hold of her by the shoulders to get her full attention and had leaned forward to whisper in her right ear, say:

"Jennifer, you and I are in the wind now, we're adrift with almost no one to trust or rely upon."

. . .

It was Sunday, July 7, the day after Taj and Natasha had exhausted their twenty dive tanks. They had just dropped anchor over Itzamal Reef when they saw Chel coming out to the *Zak Be* with fresh tanks. More delightful was when he told them the Akumal Maya had given the lovers names. Chel said that because Natasha serenaded the dawn, her name in Maya meant "Dawn Song" and that because Taj did yoga on the bowsprit, his name meant "Bridge Beyond the Light."

Natasha said, "How did you learn that way over here in Cozumel, Chel?"

"The Hand Behind the Wind told us," Chel said, giving her his broad smile, the one that showed he liked people. "There are words in His music."

. . .

It was after a dive now and the lovers could see the wind rippling the Maya blue water. This sight made them again believe they had new vision, an ability to see beyond the "breath upon the mirror." It was also further proof how diving allowed them to return here to the surface with something *more*.

75

There were purple butterflies in Taj's brillo-like, sun-bleached hair and bees on his nose. There was a smile on Natasha's face and in her eyes. Her hand was on his hip and they lay as new lovers do in their Maya blue matrimonial-size hamaca strung beneath the tarp between the forestay and the main. There, two days before the new moon, it marveled Natasha to actually *see* the wind. She was mulling over the wonder of such a thing when she heard Taj begin to hum. Natasha recognized it as a song Taj had been writing and leaned over to whisper in his ear:

"Que tal, y'all."

. . .

It was Wednesday, July 10. Having both just dreamed about bees and hummingbirds, Taj and Natasha were drawn into what tourists call "the jungle." La maya, however, called it *la selva*—the forest. La selva was a chattering loud cacophony as it seemed every avian was chattering away in screeching bird-speak: "Intruder alert! Intruder alert!" Taj and Natasha were beneath a ceiba, la selva's tallest tree and sacred to la maya. La maya called it "The World Tree" and believed it had its roots in the Underworld and its upper branches in heaven. Taj and Natasha were studying not the ceiba tree but a flower's fragile secret. The flower whose fragile secrets they were studying was an orchid living on a liana vine that had wound itself around the trunk of the ceiba. The fragile secret Taj and Natasha were studying was the orchid being poked by the long thin beak of a hummingbird at the same time a bee was partaking of some of the orchid's fragrant pollen.

"Maybe you and I can pollinate the orchid that is the world," Natasha said.

And like a light bulb coming on in his head, her words set Taj to thinking of the birds and the bees and the United States Government.

. . .

In Mayaluum Taj and Natasha ate Yucatecan food: *pollo pibil, cochinita pibil* and *t'kin'xik,* dishes spiced with achiote then wrapped

76

in banana leaves, baked in a pit and served with cilantro and Maya salsa known as *x'ni pec*—"dog's runny nose." And though the mamey, mango, papaya, pineapple, green oranges and finger-size bananas did not look so good, they had fine flavor. The jicama, chaya, tomatoes and black beans and other veggies were delicious, too. Taj and Natasha even learned to "cook" with limes, too, to make *ceviche*. Maybe best of all was keeping a hive of Yucatan's stingless bees in a hollow log to harvest their honey, honey said to be exported worldwide to enhance the flavor of other honey.

The lovers also began to grasp xutan, to feel an event before it happened.

But mostly they got wet as often as the laws of physics would allow them to dive Itzamal Reef. Just strap on an air tank and down into the Maya blue to meld with the world which had spawned life on this planet. In the Octopus's Garden they made friends with not only the octopus but a sea cucumber, a grandaddy conch and a male sea horse in whose pouch the babies were carried.

. . .

They knew it was Saturday, July 13, because Chel had told them that on this day Nacho would reappear on Isla Cozumel. During siesta that day up popped the Cozumel Maya daykeeper to power-kick out of the water to a seated position on the dive platform. He removed his mask, fins and the backpack with his tank and regulator then grabbed the aft stay so as to pull himself over the transom and lifeline. Dropping down into the cockpit and seeing Taj and Natasha sprawled out in their Maya blue hamaca between the mast and forestay, he said:

"I am another like yourself, yes?" Then, grinning pure Maya mischief, he said, "Want to get wet?"

. . .

It was Sunday morning, July 14, the French national holiday, Bastille Day, so known because one hundred seventy nine years ago today French people in Paris had stormed the national prison—the

77

Bastille—an event that became the symbol of the uprising that gave birth to the modern nation.

It turned out to be a day of freedom for Michael A., too.

His liberation began when Ma trudged up from downstairs to the faded red couch and from her apron pocket brought out the Slinky and said, "Mona-Rain-Shadow-White-Rain and I have concluded you should use this Slinky so as to let your inner child rekindle your sense of purpose. In other words: roll with Life's punches. You should also consider it an early birthday present since me'n the church ladies are leaving today for a weeklong retreat in Kerrville."

Later that morning, Michael A. took the Slinky with him when he went out to the front porch to collect the newspaper. The paper was at the bottom of the porch steps, so Michael A. set the Slinky on the top step and, after a slight push to propel the Slinky into its slow motion somersault, he and the Slinky descended twelve steps together to the concrete walkway between the porch steps and the sidewalk. While bending over to pick up the newspaper and the Slinky, a pair of black, government issue shoes walked up. It was the postman.

"Uhhh," Michael A. said, standing up, embarrassed. "Me'n Slinky here're tryin' to help my inner child rekindle my sense of purpose. See, I've sorta been at a low point in my life an' I've been languishing in self-loathing."

"Well, good luck with that," the postman said, handed over a letter and a package and left.

Michael A. frowned because personal mail was rare at 200 West 19th Street, usually just an underground magazine for Natasha called *The Rose in the Gun*. This mail was for him, Michael Antonio Medina. He opened the package first and found a pair of chan-clas—his birthday present from Nacho. Michael A. then looked at the letter and saw it was in a standard white envelope posted with a standard four-cent stamp and the return address said East Glacier, Montana. Frowning more now, Michael A. looked skyward. He was pondering who in the world he might know in East Glacier,

Montana, when seven parrots flew overhead, going north. He decided this was a good omen . . . and it was.

Because when Michael A. opened the letter and read it, it changed his life.

. . .

Reading the letter from East Glacier, Montana, left Michael A. positively incalescent. To him the letter was the parcel of a wonderful legacy. It hit him like a lightning bolt. The Fine Art of Hanging Out in the '60s was completely cast aside and replaced by Shooting Lightning Through the Sky. Two thoughts came to him. The first was a Maya-like riddle that asked "When is a uay not a uay?" and was answered with "When she's not away but right in your house." The second thought was a quote from George Washington:

> "Be courteous to all but intimate with few
> And let those few be well tried
> Before you give them your confidence."

This second thought made him wonder if his partners in Purple People Eater Productions would go along with what he had in mind.

Jack would, definitely.

Natasha would do it for the Revolution.

Taj? Yeah. He was a trooper and a good guy to have liking you.

Nacho? What Michael A. had in mind was what Nacho had always wanted for his grandson.

Same with Uncle Tunoose.

Cool Breeze would squawk, moan and groan but he would be okay with it.

But Jen would be a tough sell.

"But like my old man said," Michael A. told himself, "'Life's too short' . . . and the main aim being to amuse yourself."

Therefore it was decided by Michael A.—and only Michael A.—that not only he but all of 200 West 19th Street would be in on his shooting lightning through the sky.

Feeling propelled by his newfound sense of purpose, Michael A. was pretending he was mad as hell and not going to take it anymore.

By way of Cool Breeze's "recyclin'" and courtesy of a Gamma Sig wanting to get back at his dear old dad via a big phone bill, Michael A. now had the number of a telephone credit card. So he rode his burgundy Triumph 650 motorcycle to a pay phone at The Plantation Restaurant west of the Drag on 19th Street. There he inserted a nickel then read off the credit card's numbers to the operator and, while collecting that same nickel, said to himself: "Hamlet, Act One, Scene Three: 'Youth unto itself rebels though none else near.' Or, as Oscar Wilde said, 'The main aim is to amuse yourself.'" Then, to the party who answered the phone: "This is Marvin speaking. I don't wanta be a slacker no more, I wanta step up'n out' show ya I got a hair on my ass. I don't wanta live my life rollin' with Life's punches—I'm *rrready to rrrumble*."

"Well, it's about time," said Uncle Tunoose on the other end of the line. "Now quit hackin' your lettuce an' pack your bags—you're off to the Gold Coast."

. . .

Natasha and Taj were aboard the *Zak Be*. They were relaxing in their Maya blue hamaca and listening to Radio Havana. When the announcer said it was Wednesday, July 17, and that another United States airline had been hijacked to Cuba, Natasha turned to Taj and said:

"Hmmm, it's Michael A.'s birthday. "Wonder what he's doin.'"

. . .

On Friday, July 19, on the front porch of 200 West 19th Street, Michael A. was reading the day before's *Austin American*. He was reading about himself, about what had happened to him two days earlier. How on Wednesday, July 17, his twenty-first birthday, Cool Breeze drove him to Austin's Mueller Municipal Airport in the latter's 1956 pink Cadillac. In the trunk were two of Jen's olive green

Samsonite suitcases containing eighty pounds of pot. On Radio KNOW Donavan was singing about flying Trans-Love Airlines with Captain High as the pilot.

From Austin, Michael A. took a Trans Texas Airlines flight—aka Treetop Airlines—to Houston's Hobby Airport. From there he took National Airlines Flight 1064 bound for Fort Lauderdale. In Lauderdale Michael A. was to hook up with Mugsy for the payoff of their pot deal and, via Jen's Samsonites, continue their mutual endeavor in the underground economy.

But all did not go according to plan because martyrdom, that most sincere form of self destruction, got in the way: on that Wednesday, July 17, a Cuban named Hernandez Leyva hijacked National Airlines Flight 1064 to Cuba.

Mugsy had left Boston for Fort Lauderdale to off the one-pound bricks of what he called "ganja" because the Boston Mafia wanted a piece of any action on their turf. And this was why Michael A. was on National Airlines flight 1064 from Houston to Florida on his birthday, July 17. He was not alone on his birthday, either; he and fifty-six other passengers were aboard that DC-8 jet airliner. Michael A. was a bit miffed at himself for flying under his own name instead of using his Marvin nom de guerre. He was pondering if he could get away with "John Jacob Flugelheimer Smith" on the return flight when he heard a fellow passenger say to the stewardess:

"Take this plane to Cuba."

Right away Michael A. had a sinking feeling that he was somewhere over Missouri. No Trans-Love Airlines. No Captain High for a pilot. No, the guy now running the show was a hijacker—another stupid human trick. The guy said he had a hand grenade that could blow the DC-8 to smithereens if the plane was not diverted to Jose Marti National Airport in Havana, Cuba.

So now, two days later, Friday, July 19, Michael A. was on the front porch of the 19th Street house. He was sprawled in a purple butterfly chair and reading what yesterday's *Austin American* had to say about the hijacking. He read how the hijacker's "weapon" was a can of Old Spice shaving cream wrapped up in a dark sock and that the hijacker got a hero's welcome when he got off the plane holding up his can of Old Spice. It was the seventh hijacking to Cuba of a passenger plane this year.

"I didn't see nothin'," Michael A. had told the FBI those two days earlier. It helped that he was a United States Army veteran recently released from his military obligation due to having recently become a sole surviving son. Thus Michael A. kept his appointment with Mugsy in Fort Lauderdale and, after presenting Mugsy with the latest *Furry Freak Brothers* comic, collected what the sixteen grand he was owed for their initial pot deal up in Boston. When—after expenses—this 16K was added to the 16K down payment in that Boston alley between Big Al's Place and Little Joe's Bar, the profit was twenty-seven thousand dollars, half of which, less $500 in expenses—and something for Cool Breeze—added up to $13,000 for Michael A.

Naturally, in view of recent events, Michael A. did not fly home.

Especially with all that moolah burning a hole in his pockets.

What he did: he gave himself a belated birthday present. He got Mugsy to take him to a dealership on Broward Avenue where, for $4663, he bought a brand new metallic blue Chevrolet Corvette Stingray. Next he let Mugsy talk him into buying a solid gold Dunhill cigarette lighter and a seventeen jewel Bulova gold wrist watch. That night he and Mugsy paid a visit to the Lavender Thrill Gang, a house of ill repute where Michael A. had his ashes hauled—and his godawful ugly toes curled—by *una cubanita se llama* Graciela.

Now, Friday morning, July 19—after taking the Vette on the longest road trip of his short life—Michael A. was back home. He had just put what was left of the 16K from Mugsy in the three lock box and now he was in a purple butterfly chair reading the newspaper. He noted that the *Austin American* masthead proclaimed the newspaper to be "Read by the Decision-Makers of Texas." He thought ten cents a copy was pricey, but the $3.50 a month for both the morning *American* and the afternoon *Statesman* that Taj was laying out was a decent deal.

"Good ol' Taj," Michael A. said, "is a good guy to have liking you."

Then Michael A. read that James Earl Ray was being extradited from London to Memphis for the murder of Martin Luther King. He saw where the people in charge of the United States Post Office wanted to close 10,000 of the smallest post offices but Capitol Hill was opposed. He also read that Ronnie Raygun was getting the support of the Utah delegation's eight votes for president at the Republican National Convention. He had a visceral reaction when he read that nineteen Americans were visiting Cuba on a tour out of Spain and that they were said to be the first American tourists to visit that country since diplomatic relations were suspended between Cuba and the USA in 1961. He read that comedian-activist Dick Gregory was going off a fast, that the weather would be partly cloudy with light to moderate southerly winds and temperatures would range from the mid-seventies to the low nineties. He saw that *Camelot* was still at the Americana Theatre on Hancock Drive, that *Dr. Sex* was at the adults only Capri, *The Graduate* at the Southwood, *The Thomas Crown Affair* at The State, *Planet of the Apes* at The Austin, *The Odd Couple* at The Fox on Airport Boulevard. Also on Airport Boulevard he saw where Culp's Super Foodland had some pretty good bargains, that you could get ten pounds of potatoes there for 59 cents and fryers for 29 cents a pound. Sage on Airport and Big Bear's at 310 South Congress had some good deals, too, and all the A&P's were having double plaid stamp days. He thought of Wiley and Beep Beep when he read that H.E.B on South Congress had cans of dog food for five cents each . . .

. . . and, my oh my, at Handy Andy you could get a six pack of Milwaukee's Best for seventy-nine cents.

Import Motors at 3520 North Lamar had a 1960 Austin Healy at a good price, only $2200.

Cabaniss Brown Furniture was having a bedroom suite sale, and that big fella on TV, Oscar Snowden at 417 Congress, had some color televisions he would like to move.

One Life To Live was on at 2:30 on Channel 12. *The Edge of Night* did not interest him. Art Linklater's *House Party* came on at one in the afternoon and then there were game shows aplenty on that new UHF channel, Channel 42: *The Dating Game, The Newly-wed Game, The Hollywood Squares. The Match Game* was on later in the afternoon.

"So much to do, so little time," Michael A. said to himself as he set down the newspaper. "I wanta see Steve McQueen in *The Thomas Crown Affair* buuut"—sighing—"I gotta deal with those fifty kilos of pot Nacho dropped off with Cool Breeze while I was on the Gold Coast and turning fifty kilos into a hundred pounds without making too much shake won't be easy."

"'Acapulco Gold' is what Cool Breeze called it," he said with a sneer. "Who in the world thought of that one?"

Chapter Seven

It was Saturday, July 20, and, figuring his Gamma Sig's credit card was too hot for his purposes, Michael A. was using a new site from which to phone Uncle Tunoose: the basement of the Student Union. It was a bit public, being in the hallway by the door to the upstairs stairway and at the entrance to the bowling lanes and the pool hall. But the cords of the two phones here were long enough to be held together. So Michael A. placed the mouthpiece of one phone to the ear piece of the other then fooled the long distance operator into believing the correct change had been deposited into the pay phone the operator was on rather than the second phone. So now, after pulling down the "Coin Return" lever and pocketing that correct change, Michael A. was listening to his uncle say:

"Bein' locked up in the Big House is like accidentally tearin' off the scab of a skin cancer. It bleeds some but what pain there is you don't feel, really, until it's too late 'cause it's a silent killer what goes deep down inside you to eat away at your vitals. Flies love it though. They'll pester you by landing on it an' treat it like it's German chocolate cake. Regular hog heaven to flies it is, skin cancer." Then he snorted a phlegmy grunt and said, "The Big House ain't bad for an aging pool parlor dude such as me. I get three hots a day and a cot and they put me to work in the library."

Michael A. said, "How long are you in for?"

"I'm working on that." Then: "It's not the years or the mileage on an old jalopy like me as much as it's the takeoffs and the landings—life is compromise, life is timing . . . life is slow death. So say la maya."

"So say la maya."

"Listen, nephew, I don't want no loose ends this time of my life, see? So ya gotta clean up the proceeds—no witnesses, no crime, see? No conspicuous consumption, no talismans of the leisure class. I been readin' Thorsten Veblen's *Theory of the Leisure Class* an' also about planned obsolescence an' how everything's made to be broken—there'll be none of that, see?"

"Check. No deploying a product with a limited useful life just so it'll become unfashionable or obsolete—even though in our Throwaway Society we know full well that nothin' lasts forever."

"Just another stupid human trick," Uncle Tunoose said.

"Also vintage Furry Freak Brothers, Uncle."

. . .

It was Sunday, July 21. At four in the morning Michael A. was in the hamaca in the Crow's Nest. He was watching the street sweeper slowly motor east on the other side of 19th Street. His only company was Hannah atop the red brick chimney. At 5:30 a.m. Michael A., still in his hamaca, watched the paperboy bicycling west on the sidewalk while simultaneously folding today's paper before tossing it onto the front porch. At first light Michael A. rolled out of his hamaca, slipped into his chanclas and went downstairs, through the house and out the front door to collect the newspaper. Upon re-entering the house, newspaper under his left arm, he closed the front door behind him and walked through the entryway then the living room and dining room. In the kitchen, before going out the back door, he grabbed his Judy Jetson lunchbox chock full of tuna fish sandwiches plus a thermos filled with Superior Dairies Homogenized Milk. Now in the driveway, he looked in on Cool Breeze sawing logs in the back seat of his 1956 pink Cadillac. In the garage Michael A. opened the trunk of his now not-so-brand-spanking-new-metallic-blue Corvette Stingray to see if Jen's two olive green

Samsonite bags were still there. Satisfied, he then closed the trunk and walked forward to the driver's side of the Stingray, opened the door and eased down into the driver's seat. He had placed the newspaper and the lunch box in the passenger seat and was enjoying the Stingray's new-car smell when he heard Cool Breeze say from across the driveway:

"So Mister-Hoochie-Coochie-Man-what-was-da-Man-from-Uncle Sam an' what is once again da Man from Uncle is off to plant mo' garden, huh?"

"Marvin. For these gigs I'm Marvin."

"Not Judy Jetson, huh?"

"Nope. Marvin."

"We cool," Cool Breeze said. "Bon voyage, Mister Hoo—er, Marvin—an' here's hopin' they no travel troubles fo' your criminal enterprisin.' Me, I gotta rise'n shine'n commence hoe-in' da garden, put da weeds in dat Connelly's Florist bucket I done recycled las' eve-nin' from garbage cans, one man's trash bein' another's treasure … gonna do some serious thinkin' 'bout an earth worm farm too." Then: "No risks, no riches, no loose lips sinkin' ships, ya heah?"

"Caca pasa, chachalaca."

Michael A. then inserted the latest "recycled" bootleg—"Cheap Thrills"— into the eight-track stereo in the dashboard and pushed "Play." Once Janis broke into "Summertime," he started the engine …

… and, like Janis was singing on the eight track stereo, hoped the living would be easy on the newest, longest road trip of his life.

· · ·

Nacho was saying that this Bridge of Sighs dive would make them realize that Itzamal Reef was indeed "a sacred place where strange forces were at work."

As soon as Nacho said, "The Bridge of Sighs lies 210 feet below us," both Taj and Natasha understood that their bodies and courage were to be tested by drift-diving so far down in the Gulf Stream, the great current la maya called the River of Time. Diving at depth required near perfect execution as heavy-duty physics were involved:

your tank's 80 cubic feet of air—already compressed to 3000 pounds pressure per square inch on the surface—would be a seventh of this volume at 210 feet. Yet you still inhaled the same amount as on the surface, so at 210 feet down you had but seven minutes of bottom time.

Not counting the usual dangers—equipment failure, diver error, panic, being eaten or poisoned—there were three ways to die.

One was the bends. Decompression sickness. The seven times the usual amount of nitrogen you took in at 210 feet built up in your body tissue and blood vessels and had to exit one's body via normal respiration. Exceeding depth and time limits meant paralysis, even death. You had to know exactly how far to ascend from your maximum depth before leveling off to decompress long enough to dissolve the excess nitrogen's toxicity. Then you had to repeat the process, keep on doing so till you were within the prescribed safety limits for surfacing.

The second danger was that you had to make sure you did not exhaust your air supply trying to avoid the first danger. You had to stay calm, breathe deeply and slowly and hope you were in good enough shape to make it.

The third danger was coming up too fast. Doing so got you an embolism that would kill you in five minutes. Or sooner.

. . .

As Nacho peered overboard, sighting in, he said what his son Chel had said:

"Diving is like dancing, being *harmonious* with the current in order to feel the rhythm in your bones."

Next he inserted his mouthpiece and, after a nod to his gods, did a header off the platform.

Taj and Natasha were right behind him, each entering the water with a giant step. Thinking: Here we go through the looking glass then struck as always by the soothing silence and the freedom of weightlessness. Their heads were on swivels: looking up at the surface, out to sea then to shore, down at their long shadows on the white sand bottom, everything they saw magnified 25%. Up ahead, Nacho was streaking on a downward, westerly slant with powerful fin kicks. His arms were at his sides, his body aimed at a 60-degree angle and making a beeline for the depths so as to save air for the time-consuming ascent. Nacho was like a falcon on an attack dive, his scream the stream of bubbles shooting out his double-hose regulator's exhaust. Taj and Natasha were trying to fly like falcons, too, also kicking hard, having no problem equalizing their ears in depth's added pressure.

But neither's wings were a match for the falcon.

The divers were down to two atmospheres now—33 feet—and still over the sand field covering the island's shelf. Nacho waved at two dolphins off to the right then—*zoom*—dove right by them, over the ridge of coral that was Itzamal Reef and down the drop-off wall that was the eastern rim of the channel. While hurtling down this gray-green wall, Nacho began to follow a strip of sand there by placing this white path ten feet off his belly's beam.

The lovers were staying close behind and holding their own, also keeping their bodies straight and streamlined so as to maintain the least resistance.

By now the divers were descending into liquid blue infinity. The River of Time was like a broom sweeping the depths so clean there was almost unlimited visibility. Right now they were crossing the threshold where colors grow fainter; they were entering what divers call the Twilight Zone. Here the drop-off wall had no coral, just an expanse of sea ivy. Looking up, Taj saw the wall as a cliff and knew that without it as a reference point he would have succumbed to the optical illusion that the surface was only a few feet away.

The lovers positioned themselves off Nacho's left shoulder and this allowed his bubble trail to graze the top of their heads as they tacked down through the River of Time. At a depth of 100 feet everyone arched their backs and pulled out of their attack dives to level off as the white path led them onto a precipice extending 50 feet out from the drop-off to where the path ended, became the north fork of a colorful crossroads.

To the crossroads' east was a trail of red deep-water gorgonians, a corridor of yellow tube sponges led south while, to the west, was a blackness neither Taj nor Natasha could fathom. The crossroads' nexus was a colony of elkhorn coral resembling a tree about ten feet tall, and in the muted lighting this tree of flowering rock appeared blue-green—Maya blue, the color of the divine. The shadows Taj saw fluttering in its upper branches were another optical illusion, shadows of surface ripples. Yet Taj was mindful he could be wrong as he was now within the realm of nitrogen narcosis: rapture of the deep. Being "narked-out" made you tipsy, squeezed your awareness away till you did not know which way was up. Taj, who had read you were only half as smart at 100 feet when narked-out, each now began to wonder:

Just how smart am I gonna be at 210 feet?

Taj was wondering this when he saw Nacho stop on a floating dime down current from the tree, hover there until Taj and Natasha came up behind him, kicking to stay in place. Nacho then kicked once and fell like a leaf, spiraling around the tree as he did so—leaving Taj amazed at how he could go against the current with so little effort. But then, nearing the tree, Taj felt the same sensation that Nacho had: the force that lived there pulling him—and Natasha—down and around the tree. Taj figured the red-yellow-white-black crossroads must be where three currents met, where two finger currents of the River of Time rejoined the mother force. The eddy spawned by the merger of these energies was the force that allowed a diver to spiral down and around the tree.

Using the eddy was a move neither Taj nor Natasha would have thought of, made the lovers realize that Nacho, by being "harmonious so as to feel the rhythm in your bones," had a different slant on logic, was smart in ways they had yet to learn.

When the lovers joined Nacho west of the coral tree, they saw the blackness there was a vertical shaft six feet in diameter. Nacho now disappeared into the shaft—only to poke his head out and exhale an air ring before ducking back in. This air ring briefly lassoed the lovers as it rose, expanding as the pressure within it was reduced. Taj guessed it would be seven to ten feet in diameter when it broke the surface.

As the lovers entered the shaft in tandem, Natasha banged her tank on the top of the entrance, but Nacho merely looked back: a quick glance before going on. Not inquiring if she was okay, but gauging her composure by her eyes—which were not wide with fear, just intrigued by a cave behind the tiny branches of black coral in the shaft.

Nacho was now nearing the sphere of azure blue that was the exit. The lovers were following, intrigued by three caves in the shaft's walls. Their depth gauges now said 150 feet, so they wondered if the Bridge of Sighs was at the end of the 100-foot shaft as that would be 200 feet deep.

Natasha was also starting to wonder if Nacho had a death wish.

Taj was wondering this, too, as Nacho exited the shaft to reenter the blue wilderness below the precipice's 100-foot-shaft. There Nacho emerged into a tower of soft, blue-green light made by the afternoon sun shining down through the shaft. In this surreal glow Nacho seemed to shine as well as he waited for Taj and Natasha with his legs crossed Indian style at the ankles, arms extended to his knees, each thumb and forefinger clasped in a circle. He was floating in this full lotus within blue infinity beside a natural bridge.

The Bridge of Sighs dive had now become a slow waltz.

. . .

There was no current below the shaft, just dead calm. Nacho was still in his full lotus, Taj and Natasha beside him and Taj thinking he must be narked-out because Nacho reminded him of the hookah-puffing caterpillar in *Alice in Wonderland*. The one whose smoke rings had said to Alice: *Who ... are ... you?*

Nacho was grinning around his mouthpiece, totally at ease as he exhaled more air rings, the rings exploding as they collided with the underside of the precipice to dislodge silt that had accumulated there over the millennia. The silt seemed neon in the eerie lighting, twinkling like blue-green fairy dust as it cascaded around and over the lovers, who were now having to work hard just to breathe. Their air supply was so compressed—seven times as much—that it lumbered through their regulator hoses before rumbling with a low roar into their mouthpieces. Once they had exited the shaft they noted that the arrow on their depth gauges was at its limit, 200 feet. Now Taj and Natasha took personal readings and decided they did not feel narked-out—yet reminded themselves that it could fool you, that it was supposed to be a pretty sneaky phenomenon.

Actually, they both believed that, if they were dead, this must be heaven because they knew of no place like it on earth.

The lovers now took in their surroundings. A few feet above them was the precipice that housed the shaft they had recently exited. Using his compass, Taj noted that to the west was the dark blue of the Cozumel Channel. Behind them—east—the drop-off wall ran north for as far as Taj could see in the limited lighting below the precipice. Immediately to the south they could again see the Bridge of Sighs. It was a natural bridge about 30 feet long, a straight limestone span over a cleft that extended into blue oblivion down the drop-off wall. Just beyond it the drop-off wall curved eastward into the north face of a cliff.

Despite the apparent absence of current some kind of force now propelled Nacho, still in his full lotus, across the Bridge of Sighs to that cliff face in the drop-off wall. There, with his bubble trail dislodging more silt, Nacho broke from the lotus and began to hang vertically in front of a dark spot in the wall.

Both Taj and Natasha now saw that the dark spot was the mouth of another cave, so each lover reached for the other's hand.

Taj saw this cave mouth as like the one in the cliff face in the movie *King Kong*—the mountain lair where Kong stashed Fay Wray. Through no conscious will of their own Taj and Natasha now found themselves crossing the Bridge of Sighs. Once drawn to the other side, with the fairy dust from Nacho's bubbles sprinkling down over them, they saw Nacho strike the pose of the Jaguar Warrior.

And as he danced the Dance of the Jaguar Warrior, it was then that Taj and Natasha saw the cave mouth in the cliff face come alive.

The lovers hung with the moment, watching in awe as the mouth seemed to gape, twist and grow into a gigantic maw of contorted lips and snarling teeth. To them it was as though the cave had indeed become King Kong's mouth. Taj told himself that this was merely another underwater optical illusion.

And when Nacho broke the pose, the monstrous maw went away.

Now, as all three divers hovered shoulder to shoulder above the cave mouth's lower lip, they held hands and admired the view. Here was the ideal spot to get the big picture: Cozumel's base—the drop-off—was like a 3000-foot-tall tree trunk, the reefs its branches, the island the tree's crown. Though the lovers were unable to see the bottom, in the deep blue peace of the soft blur that was the edge of visibility they could make out a swirling, G-shaped nebula. Gradually, this G-shape came into focus as five conga lines of life forms. These life forms were stretched end-to-end, nose to wing-tipped tail and revolving counter-clockwise around a common center.

Nacho waved at them, so Taj and Natasha did, too.

And it was then that Taj realized they were seeing a pod of dolphins.

And it was also then that Taj felt a long lost feeling.

. . .

On that dive, when Taj was holding hands with Nacho and Natasha at 210 feet beneath the sea, where the ambient pressure was seven times greater than on the surface, what Taj had felt was a throb in his throat. This throb pulsed through his body from head to toe. Long before this dive, Taj had been left speechless by a childhood trauma—but when he surfaced, Natasha could see a new aura had gathered around Taj. The new aura was there because Taj knew that he could speak again.

Nacho saw Taj's new aura, too, and wise man that he was, he left the lovers alone by scurrying up onto the dive platform and back aboard the *Zak Be*. Left floating beside each other in the Maya blue warmth of the sea a few yards astern, the first words Taj had spoken in years were expressed only for Natasha and as naturally as the breath that brought those words. He said:

"Que tal, y'all?"

The moment so completely disarmed Natasha that from within her radiated a smile as pure and beautiful as any sunrise. A glorious smile that made Taj say:

"You are the sun to me and you make me feel like the moon as it basks in your light."

"That's nice ... but it's also pretty corny."

Taj's new aura then took on a hint of mischief and he said, "Methinks my revolutionary has a wee eensy snitch of anarchist in her, yes?"

. . .

Back aboard the *Zak Be* after that dive Nacho announced that Taj and Natasha's journey of discovery in Mayaluum, this bold blessing of their love, was set to end: he, Chel, Taj and Natasha would sail the *Zak Be* north, from the Straits of Yucatan to Galveston Bay.

What sailors call a "crossing" or "passage."

. . .

They no longer knew the day of the week nor the date, and they did not care.

Today they had again gone down thirty feet to the sand, to their underwater heaven. Their happiness was ubiquitous: from head to toe, from mask to fin, their auras glowed like halos with symbiotic joy as they communed with the octopus, the sea cuke, the grandaddy conch and the sea horse. These denizens of the depths, the divers believed, saw them as blessed angels come down to steward the sea because Taj and Natasha were making sure the anchor and its chain did not destroy the homes of these sea critters. The divers also policed the white sand of Itzamal Reef by picking up whatever garbage the River of Time trudged in. Always looking after all their marine brethren, on this day they rescued the planet's biggest fish caught in fishing net. Without a knife it took a while to free the whale shark but throughout the rescue the big beast helped by remaining calm. It was such a relief to see the whale shark swim away and resume its yearlong circumnavigation of the globe, its monstrous mouth wide again open and feeding on the plankton it filtered from the tons of water passing through its 40-foot body.

Later, in their Maya blue hamaca strung between the forestay and the main, for the first time they talked of who they were before they had met. Taj had begun by saying, "I once counted thirty-two private schools that had me for a student."

"All tears are the same," Natasha said. "I went to four public schools and I got thrown out of all four." She told Taj that she never knew who her real parents were, that all the man who raised her had ever said was that he had found her abandoned. Natasha said that she and "Daddy" lived on some acreage four miles northwest of Jollyville on a diet that was mostly chicken eggs and goat's milk.

Taj said, "I was raised on all the foods in the world because I was never in one place for more than a few weeks."

Natasha said, "Daddy was a cedar chopper. Selling firewood was pretty much all the cash that came into our lives. Mostly we survived on handouts—alms for the poor. Daddy never really worked for anyone but God. He was what they call 'on the Word'—-he was a street corner preacher. We'd hitchhike into town and get dropped off at the southwest corner of 23rd and the Drag. Daddy would start waving his Bible and preaching the Word while I sang "Jesus Wants Me for a Sunbeam.""

Taj said, "My parents and almost all my extended family were in the diplomatic service of one government or another and because of this …" Here he stopped talking and pointed to his throat, Natasha understanding that he was referring to the childhood trauma that took his voice. "Because of this my mother and I were estranged from my father and were shuffled from one relative to another. Whenever I saw my father he would only say that he was proud of my academic record … Mother spent her whole life cooing and reminding me that I was 'special.' I have often wondered if they were my real parents."

Natasha said, smiling again, "So I guess you are what Jen says you are—'Everyman'."

. . .

It was dawning Tuesday, July 23. They would soon set sail so as to take their leave of this Paradise called Mayaluum. Right now Natasha was standing at the Maya blue water's edge. There was no surf. The Cozumel Channel was as calm as a bathtub. So was la selva. Natasha was looking down at her bare feet and watching the white sand foam up from beneath her soles to seep over her feet, become icky toe jam. She was watching this from within the silent presence of cloud serpents—what la maya called the fingers of fog coming off the Cozumel Channel. Abruptly, a loud snap of motion came from la selva, quite possibly the breaking of undergrowth by a creature as big as she. The noise caused Natasha to look up and wonder if that was a black-as-night jaguar darting out from la selva to disappear into the cloud serpents' milky mists. But she knew that she could not be certain of this because by now she had learned that nothing was what it seemed down here in Mayaluum. And this was what made Natasha next wonder, as Father Sun came out to dismiss, shoo away the cloud serpents, if she were actually witnessing a calamity of events among The Forces That Are.

For now it seemed that two of The Forces That Are—the trade wind from the southwest and the shore wind from the northeast—had forged a crossfire, a crossroads of elements. It seemed that these elements were rubbing against one another in the heavens above Where the Sky Is Born—and here ashore, too, for it seemed the two winds' progeny of a new wind was making ripples in the sand beneath her feet. Natasha now saw the union of these two winds being forceful out on the water, too, by meeting up with the River of Time to throw up a stationary wave out there, erect a two-foot-high white ripple of foam that resembled the ripples of white sand at her feet. And when Natasha looked up above her at the clear tropical sky, she could see this blue sky now being rippled by a long white stratus cloud scudding north.

Seeing this calamity of events as illustrating a ripple effect, to herself Natasha said, "As is earth and sky so is sea: one planet, one world!" And in this moment Natasha heard The Forces That Are harmonizing with that new wind.

And she saw the music it was making.

. . .

Taj was saying, "It is hard to imagine much less find a simpler place in Time."

Natasha said, "Here in this Mayaluum we move like the sea, you and I."

"We have seen the sunrise from the bottom of the sea."

"Rainbows too," she said.

"And I have felt you like I never felt me."

It was then that the hiss of a falling coconut broke the spell.

. . .

They were setting sail. The anchor had been raised then the jib. It was time to say goodbye. Natasha was feeling the lingering sadness of bidding adieu to a place that had transformed her. Her heart had fallen in love with Mayaluum.

But now, for at least five days—and for twenty-four hours a day—it would be four folks at sea and that meant close quarters for the crew of the 42' *Zak Be.*

Especially for Natasha because she was the only woman.

Right now Natasha was seated in the cockpit, her head turned over her right shoulder, her chin resting on the stern rail so she could look astern at Cozumel Island. As Chel and Taj now raised the mainsail so that the *Zak Be* heeled over to starboard, Natasha was seeing Cozumel Island as one of Mother Nature's larger than life jewels: an emerald with a necklace of white powder sand set within the shimmering turquoise that was the shallows and all of that set against the deep blue body of the Caribbean Sea.

Turning to look forward, she saw Nacho at the helm and, like everybody else aboard, wearing little more than a smile. He was

97

setting a course north for the open sea, his feet spread in a confident stance, arms extended so that his hands held full command of the polished teak helm. Chel, meanwhile, had gone forward to the bowsprit to look back at his island. Taj now came up to stand beside Natasha and, as always, was exuding his quiet way. Both his nut brown body and his sun-bleached frizzy hair seemed to beam back at the sun.

Natasha now turned once again toward the island. She could not take her eyes from the seven-story Hotel Tulan. She saw it as a modern Maya pyramid: its west side step-sided as it rose up from the water's edge for six floors, each higher floor not as big as the floor below it. The seventh and top floor—the penthouse—was like a bridge to the six floors on the east, la selva's side. She now realized that the Tulan's shape was meant to symbolize the thirteen levels of Maya heaven.

Looking down at Itzamal Reef now and recalling the 200' dive with Nacho, Natasha now realized that Itzamal Reef symbolized Maya hell's nine levels: down four levels then one level across and four up.

"As is sea so is earth and sky," she said, and right away heard Taj's new voice say:

"Que tal, y'all?"

Neither had a clue that the bulk of the *Zak Be's* cargo—5000 pounds worth—was contraband.

Chapter Eight

July 24, 1968, was Jack's birthday.

Jen started off her man's twenty-first birthday with his favorite breakfast of pancakes. No electricity in the home place meant milk would not keep, so Jen improvised: she used club soda.

Mother Nature's first birthday present to Jack was a cool morning—only eighty degrees. Jack took advantage of this cool weather to do a chore of development: tear down the abandoned pig shed beyond the kitchen patch. Actually, this chore had been Jen's idea, more of her "woman's touch." While doing so, Jack happened upon some family history: he found his Granma Gage's cast iron Dutch oven, a box of votivo candles from the candle factory in Alpine plus more of Granpa Gage's whittled slingshots and a cache of his 1930s *Saturday Evening Post*.

The real treasure, though, was a dusty Charles Dickens *A Tale of Two Cities* . . . and when Jack pried open the cover with a finger, there on the fly leaf, he found a treasure that brought a lump of angst into his throat. An inscription that read:

> *To my Ben Jack for his first ever train ride*
> *Love,*
> *Lydia . . . May, 1910*

At noon that Wednesday, July 24, Mother Nature served up a second birthday present: rain. It rained not long but hard. It rained so hard that, according to Jack, Granpa Gage would have said, "It done come a real turd-floater."

Jen, of course, was more politically correct, saying, "It's the onset of monsoon season."

By sunset the rain had turned the ocotillo fence into just what Jack had predicted it would be: "right pretty." The five-foot high ocotillo stalks had turned green and were abloom with small scarlet flowers. In the twilight, amid the agaves, desert candles and yuccas about the home place, the scarlet of the ocotillo fence and the red of the Saltillo tile roof brought jewel-like color to this part of the badlands. Jack's chores of development and the woman's touch that was Jen were making Rancho Quien Sabe appear downright prosperous.

For his birthday that evening Jen gave Jack, first, a party. It was not their dream date at Green Pastures Restaurant back in Austin, but it was all the lovers wanted. For the occasion Jen wore a jean skirt, a peasant blouse and Granma's Gage's Nocona boots. Jack wore his Mexican wedding shirt and, as usual, cutoffs and his Granpa's Lucchese boots. A second gift from Jen was a chocolate cake. She had used Yucatecan honey in lieu of sugar and baked it in their Dutch oven. After she placed a votivo candle atop the cake then lighted it, she told Jack to make a wish. When he had blown out the candle, Jack said his wish was to own a farm up on the Caprock.

Later, Jen sat Jack down in their hamaca and stood behind him as she took down his pony tail to braid his hair. Afterwards, Jack did something that had been a long time coming: he shaved with Granpa Gage's straight razor. As this was happening, Mother Nature brought yet another gift: a rare blue norther that usurped the southwest wind and tumbled the temperature twenty degrees in fifteen minutes. This norther sent tumbleweeds dancing from north to south and spawned seven remolinos.

Around those seven remolinos Jack and Jen's seemingly ubiquitous pair of peregrine falcons flew figure eights.

And as the lovers looked up at the falcons a sliver of a feather fell down from above, tumbling toward them slowly like an autumn leaf until it came to rest in Jack's hair.

"Well, I'll swan," Jack said, shaking his head in disbelief. "It's the tail feather of a peregrine falcon,"

"Happy birthday from your uay, hon."

. . .

Later it was someone else's birthday that July 24, 1968.

In the cool of the norther, around ten o'clock, Jack was out on the front porch tuning his Mexican six string guitar and Jen was out back seated in the rainbow-colored matrimonial-size hamaca in the kitchen patch. She was shucking ears of corn when she heard the sound of something scratching. Tiptoeing through the moonlight, Jen discovered that the scratching sound was coming from one of the brown eggs used for the club soda pancakes. Moving closer, Jen saw that one of those eggs was being pecked open from the inside. Next a teeny-weeny beak appeared and Jen heard:

"Cheep!"

After going over to examine the situation, Jen's maternal instincts kicked in. She cracked open another brown egg and, using an eye dropper, gave the teeny-weeny beak some egg goo. It was not long before the goo strengthened the motherless chick sufficiently for a break though, and out came a golf-ball-sized puff of fuzz sporting two spindly toothpick-sized pink legs and a pink beak.

"Cheep!"

That night the chick stayed warm on Jen's her shoulder by roosting there in her hair. After every "*cheep!*" the dogs would prick their ears beneath Jack and Jen's hamaca then tilt their heads to one side to look up intently at Jack and Jen.

"If this don't beat all I ever saw," Jack said. "Jen, you're a Mother Hen—you're Mother Hen Jen."

"Oh, hush. Boo Boo's nice and warm under my hair and this way our little Boo Boo's protected from Mr. Bullsnake—and don't forget you and Boo Boo share a birthday."

"Goldurned thing better be a laying hen or it'll be supper pretty quick."

"Of course Boo Boo will be a laying hen—and she won't *ever* be supper, Ben Jack Gage. I'm putting my foot down about any notion of Boo Boo ever being anybody's supper."

"Yes, ma'am." Then: "Boo Boo, huh?"

. . .

Later on the night of his birthday, in their rainbow-colored matrimonial-size hamaca strung up in the kitchen patch, Jen squeezed Jack and said:

"Once again I gotcha surrounded, don't I, Cowboy?"

"Yes'um, Cowboy's sure enough surrounded all right." Sigh. "Now do what you will with Cowboy, purty please."

"Gotcha covered."

"Cheep!"

. . .

Not long after Jack's birthday, during a Big Bend sunset, Jen was like Mr. Bullsnake: merely another long shadow among the desert's earth tones as she slipped into the privy. Next, while lowering her cutoffs and gotchees, but before squatting, she uttered her usual incantation of "When in Rome." Then down she went to strike the pose of Rodin's The Thinker. The pose cleared her mind. But of course it helped that Wiley and Beep Beep sat like sentinels on each side of this enclosed throne. It also helped that Jen's "woman's touch" had persuaded Jack to nail to the privy's south wall one of Granpa Gage's whittled slingshots as a toilet paper holder thus no more fumbling around in the dark with her hand exposed.

It also helped to hear the "*Cheep!*" of that little fuzzball in Jen's hair.

102

Feeling secure now, Jen looked outside and again agreed with Jack that from here was "the bestest goldurned view from a privy in South Brewster County bar *none!*" In the foreground of her view from the privy was Rancho Quien Sabe: a parched parcel of desert one mile south of Terlingua with no crops nor livestock to tend. Just a little bit of ground for living with Mother Nature and enjoying its view of Her wondrous works. Beyond the home place was Ben Jack Gage's Big Muddy Buddy. To the east was the Chisos Mountains with its centerpiece Casa Grande presiding over Emory Peak and the twin spires known as Mule Ears. To the west—and now bathed in sunset's electric lavender majesty—was the quarter-mile high, one-hundred-fifty-yard-wide mouth of Santa Elena Canyon. Buried just above his beloved river "what's too thick to drink and too thin to plow" was Granpa Gage, interred beside his wife, son and daughter-in-law.

It was there in that Big Bend sunset that Jen realized she was starting to feel the xutan of her and Jack's imminent departure from the home place.

In their time out here in the badlands Jen had seen a pair of peregrine falcons waltz around remolinos on a cold summer day. She had seen a bear sunning itself on a rock. She had seen all sorts of javelina and deer and quail and enough snakes, skunks and other critters to no longer be riled should they trespass and become "varmints." She had hung in the wind and had witnessed tumble-weeds dance to its anthem. She had become quite the flyswatter, dog doctor, Dutch oven wiz and wax-maker.

She had become Mother Hen Jen—"*Cheep!*"

Even better, she felt that she had matured as a person. Now not only did the home place appear prosperous but her and Jack's home out here in the Big Empty melded with Mother Earth. Jack and Jen's dirt structure with its red roof of Saltillo tiles and living fence, yuccas and agaves was nearly as natural in its appearance in the desert as an oasis. To Jack and Jen it *was* an oasis and, realizing this, Jen now said aloud:

"One *world*, one planet!"

She also realized that The Analuz Trail—the path that had been blazed from toting their cayuco down to the river—had become another game trail for her and Jack's fellow desert's denizens. Jack would say "Wanta see a secret?" and Jen would say "Always," and they would be off to the "Otherworld"—what Jack called Santa Elena Canyon. There he had shared with her childhood haunts: waterfalls, tinajas, *jacales,* ancient hearths and campgrounds, arrowheads and sand paintings from a lost civilization. Jack had taught her how to read sign and discern who had made the tracks and the scat that the lovers had come upon.

Jen saw her summer vacation as being like the life of an autumn leaf. Though she had hung tough in the wind, the time was approaching to fall away and return to 19th and University. Not only did the Jackass and the Jenny now have their own home but, once again, like Palenque, they had been transformed by a place. They had forged a higher love. Their Language of Touch still did not stutter, had nary a twitch nor a hitch in its get-a-long.

Jack and Jen's summer vacation of 1968 had indeed done them some justice. There had even been some closure with regard to her parents' untimely passing.

Jen's mind now turned to the future: what was next on the Road of Life? This fall she would be entering her senior year at the University and was on track to graduate in May with a Bachelor of Arts in English Literature. But then what? A girl's gotta eat. Her parents' death had left her deep in debt: their funerals and cemetery plots plus an overabundance of personal debt. A school teacher's salary offered but bare subsistence. Any other jobs for an English Lit degree were few and far between and—as she had learned at Hyde Park Recreation Club—sexism was part of life in the World of Work. And then there was Jack, and what was now Jack and her: "Forever here. Here forever. Ever forward." Right then and there Jen rose from her Thinker's pose knowing what needed to be done: make the band a success. In the meantime, she would further her education by going to graduate school. The University was affordable—$150 was the most for tuition and fees she had ever paid—and she could always keep working at the Main Library.

Besides, Life was good at 19th and University.

Relieved by this decision, her next act was to step outside the privy and begin gathering up a basket of Big Bend wild flowers for the August 1ˢᵗ return to Austin. Jen was hearing "*Cheep!*" in her left ear when she saw a southwest wind stirring the dust into a brown ground fog. It made her wonder if, since she was *seeing* the wind, then why not music as well. So she hummed a song she was working on …

And *sawww* it.

. . .

There were no travel troubles for Michael A., no bumps in his Road.

Following the instructions in the letter from Glacier National Park, he turned off Highway 82 near Aspen, Colorado, and drove to a rustic cabin on Woody Creek. Here, on the evening of July 25, Michael A. met up with Cacciatore, a tall, balding wild man who smoked Thai Sticks out of a cigarette holder and said stuff like, "Ya gotta wear the bastards down." He also told Michael A. "Your old man was solid, a standup guy."

After accepting Michael A.'s gift of the latest *Furry Freak Brothers* comic book, Cacciatore paid cash—$10K—for the fifty pounds of Acapulco Gold in one of Jen's olive green Samsonite suitcases.

Even better, later on Michael A. hooked up with an Aspen ski instructress with a golden tan and they tripped the light fantastic in The Galaxy Club at the base of Aspen Mountain. Her name was Signe and that night Michael A. did not give a rosy red rat's patoot if she cost him money and misery, even pain. And when she leaned in close to plant one fully on his lips before whispering in his ear in a lusty tone of voice: "Now use your imagination …"

… Michael A. grinned like a banshee.

. . .

It was Friday, July 26. After the two men had driven east in the Corvette on the Going-to-the-Sun Road, they stopped at the summit of Logan Pass so they could toke on a peace pipe that came out of a handwoven, beaded elkskin medicine bag. Here, to Michael A.'s delight, atop the Continental Divide at an altitude of 6846 feet, the Corvette's radio was able to pick the 50,000 watt radio station KOMA broadcasting all the way from Oklahoma City, Oklahoma. So, while listening to Otis Redding sing "Sittin' On The Dock of the Bay" and as a nearby white mountain goat paid them no attention, both men gazed down into a mountain-green, wild-flowered meadow where a bull elk was strutting his stuff for his twenty-five grazing females. As the bull elk strutted and the females grazed, Walks In Blue Green told it like this:

"Your daddy was pure D Code of the West, a straight up warrior's warrior even in The Nam. For nearly three tours of The Nam I was his sergeant and he was my captain an' him'n me went to hell'n back often. That night he got it him'n me were in the convoy's lead truck rounding a bend in the supply route. The Charlie sniper should've started the ambush by taking me out 'cause I was driving but through his scope he must've seen your daddy's captain's bars . . . got your daddy right through the windshield. The captain never knew what hit him, never heard the bullet, never saw nothin' but oblivion. I got a medal for evading the ambush by floorin' it'n drivin' on though I was deaf as a post from the blast'n had your daddy's brains splattered all over me."

Michael A. said, "War—*hah!*—what's it good for? Nothin but death an' destruction." Then: "Did the old man ever say 'This is a good day to die?' That's what Indians in the movies say before going into battle."

"No, he didn't said anything." Walks In Blue Green then patted the beaded medicine bag and said, "He did like to say, though, that mota'll getcha through times of no money better'n money'll getcha through times of no mota'."

"White man speak with forked tongue," Michael A. said.

· · ·

Walks In Blue Green's people called their land "Where the Night Sky Is Born." The United States Government called it the Blackfeet Reservation but Walks In Blue Green called it "The Rez."

"The Rez is a sovereign nation and I'm an elder in the Blackfeet Nation's Piegan tribe," Walks In Blue Green said as he and Michael A. sat Indian style around a campfire within the former's eighteen-foot-high tipi whose buffalo hide shell was painted with an ancient symbol he called"the Sacred 'G'."

It had come time to parley, so Michael A. opened Jen's other olive green Samsonite suitcase and from atop its fifty pounds of Acapulco Gold removed the latest *Furry Freak Brothers* comic book and presented it to his host. Next Walks In Blue Green handed over the handwoven, beaded elkskin medicine bag and said:

"This medicine bag is a sign of respect from my people to you. Part of what's inside it is what we agreed upon for"—pointing at the Acapulco Gold—"which we Piegans see as a sacramental substance. The rest is from your father, something he wanted you and your mother to have."

Michael A. took a peek inside the medicine bag and said, "Cheepers, Walks In Blue Green. I sure hope you ain't an Indian giver."

· · ·

So here he was: shooting lightning through the sky under a nearly full moon. Or so it seemed. On the northern horizon, above the Canadian Rockies, a lightning storm was shooting its electric energy up and down and sideways—and appeared to do so every time Michael A. nodded his head quickly and blinked his eyes just like Barbara Eden did in *I Dream of Jeannie*. Lying beneath the buffalo robe, Michael A. saw a kajillon stars above him. Beside him beneath the buffalo robe was Two Moons and the handwoven, beaded elkskin medicine bag. From where he and Two Moons were camped—a meadow high above Two Medicine Lake—they could see down to the Piegan tribe's seven tipis, each glowing red from campfires within. The dogs running free down there had Michael

107

A. thinking of Wiley and Beep Beep and, as he smelled the wood smoke from the tipi fires, he saw the tipis as seven pyramids. It had been earlier, at dusk, when Two Moons had led him here on a hike. As a gaggle of Canadian geese honked in the tall green grass of the meadow and off in the dark distance a bull elk bugled for females, Two Moons had shown him a bull moose beside a whitetail fawn and a Bohemian Waxwing sharing a tall pine with a Downy Woodpecker.

"Top of the world," he now said to himself as much as to Two Moons.

"The crown of creation atop the Crown of the Continent is what we call it," she said, nestling into his armpit with the top of her head to snuggle and cuddle.

"'Crown of the Continent'—that's the Blackfeet Indian name for Glacier National Park," Michael A. said. Then recited her tour spiel on the hike up here: "More than twenty-five glaciers, 130 lakes, 200 waterfalls, 350 grizzly bears, a million plus acres—and one helluva sweat lodge for getting it on with the oh-too-lovely Miss Two Moons."

"You're silly," she said, giggling.

"Glacier National Park," he said, continuing, "was dedicated on May 11, 1910, by none other than Teddy Roosevelt."

"Goo goo kachoo," Two Moons said, giggling some more.

"Caca pasa, chachalaca," he said, also giggling. Then he did his best Mel Blanc rendition of Marvin the Martian's voice: "Where's the kaboom?"

That night, high in the meadow above Two Medicine Lake, with no walls—and no Mona around him—Michael A. slept serene and safe beside Two Moons, his head resting on the handwoven, beaded elkskin medicine bag.

. . .

It was Sunday evening, July 28, and Michael A. was at the East Glacier train station again following instructions: taking the train to San Francisco via Portland. He had just alighted from Walks In

Blue Green's not quite brand spanking new metallic blue Chevrolet Corvette Stingray which Walks In Blue Green had just purchased for $4663 cash money from Miguel Antonio Medina. Michael A. had let the Vette go because Uncle Tunoose had read too much Thorsten Veblen in the prison and thus had ,insisted the sports car was way too much conspicuous consumption, "a talisman of the leisure class, too damned obvious."

The Piegans had treated Michael A. like visiting royalty. They had bestowed upon him elk skin moccasins and buckskin war shirts brightly beaded across the chest and with fringe on the sleeves. They had also presented Michael A. with genuine Plains Indian dance sticks, a flute, a drum, a whistle, a rattle, a walking stick and a tomahawk pipe. For grins and solidarity and brotherhood and payback and good karma, Michael A. had thrown in on the Vette deal his other talismans of the leisure class he had bought in Fort Lauderdale: the solid gold Dunhill cigarette lighter and seventeen jewel Bulova gold wrist watch.

At the train station Michael A. had checked Jen's two olive green Samsonite bags as baggage—both now stuffed with his Piegan goodies—but he was not letting his handwoven, beaded elkskin medicine out of his sight. It kept it over his shoulder and tight against his ribs.

While waiting for the train, he read the station's wall posters: old timey ones from the 1930s produced by the WPA—the Works Progress Administration—to encourage the public to see America. The poster Michael A. looked the longest at said "Half the Park Is After Dark."

Michael A. thought it should say "Where the Night Sky Is Born."

· · ·

Still following instructions, Monday, July 29, Michael A. took San Francisco municipal transportation to a sidewalk coffee house in North Beach named Enrico's. There, again following instructions, he looked for and found a guy reading Richard Brautigan's *Trout Fishing In America*. The guy was a poet named Red Fred—a distant

109

relative of Uncle Tunoose, a Lebanese American with low friends in high places back in the old country. Still following instructions, Michael A. gave Red Fred the latest *Furry Freak Brothers* comic book with a white envelope in it holding $15K cash. Red Fred responded by pushing a Monkey Ward's black briefcase up against Michael A.'s left foot and saying:

"The ten kilos of Lebanese government-stamped black hashish in the briefcase will get you through times of no money better'n money'll get you through times of no hashish."

. . .

She said her name was Li Mam and Michael A. felt right away that, like Signe and Two Moons, she was true blue, would not cost him money nor misery. Li Mam was not a typical California girl because she was neither a sun-kissed blonde nor was she fashionably lean and lame. She was head to toe one hundred percent San Francisco Chinese.

Once again following instructions, Michael A. met Li Mam Monday, July 29, atop Strawberry Hill in San Francisco's Golden Gate Park. Li Mam was nekkid as a jaybird and performing her Tai Chi routine. Michael A., too, was nekkid as a jaybird—nary a stitch between them—because the Mexamerileb from Austin was tripping on Owsley Acid—courtesy of Red Fred—and having flashes that he was Emperor Norton I, a San Francisco historical character from the previous century.

"You're erotic," Michael A. had said to Li Mam through his Owsley-glazed eyes whose pupils were dilated huuuge, practically the size of Betty Boop's.

"Erotic is that which you desire," she said.

"Emperor Norton hereby declares this to be love at first sight."

And in their next breath they got down to it.

. . .

Love is blind and money burns and, consequently, in less than twenty-four hours Michael A. blew a bundle. It was not that Li Ma was costing Michael A. money; no, it was that he was rationalizing that he was investing said bundle on behalf of Purple People Eater Productions' San Francisco branch. First he invested in another Triumph 650 motorcycle which, like the Vette, was also metallic blue. Next he rented a second floor flat on Ninth Street around the corner from Clement Street and but a block away from Golden Gate Park. The flat had two bedrooms, both with bay windows. The flat was low profile—no conspicuous consumption—and thus presumably would be acceptable to Uncle Tunoose for stashing the hashish Li Mam and her family's connections could off aplenty.

To Michael A. however, the absolute best part of the flat was the gizmo that opened the street door. It was a lever-operated gadget that let him buzz in folks down at the street entrance. Even better, it was the same gizmo as Steve McQueen had in his San Francisco digs in *Bullit*.

· · ·

With Li Mam behind him on the metallic blue Triumph 650, her arms clasped around his waist, they rode the streets of San Francisco. First they went to Haight Ashbury and the Panhandle part of Golden Gate Park where the Grateful Dead and Jefferson Airplane had houses. At the latter abode Michael A. got to strum along with David Crosby, Phil Lesh and Jack Casady. Later he and Li Mam visited Austinites Chet Helm and Gary Scanlan of the Family Dog, The Jomo Disaster Light Show's Belmer Wright, Doug Brown and Joe Fish. They also rode the Triumph along The Great Ocean Highway north to Marin County. On Stinson Beach they walked hand-in-hand on its coffee-with-cream-colored sand alongside white breakers and amid sea shells and pebbles polished smooth by the surf after having been dredged up from the Pacific Ocean's depths. They fed sea birds and beachcombed themselves a blue-green glass buoy that Li Mam said came from a Japanese fishing net. Back in the city they went to Telegraph Hill and Coit Tower, past Pacific Heights and Nob Hill mansions and Grace Memorial Church, down crooked old Lombard Street. They even walked the

Filbert Steps, the 400 wooden planks that wound up past people's homes with awesome views of the bay. Though it was summertime, it was cold, so Michael A. quoted Mark Twain:

" 'The coldest winter I ever spent was the summer I lived in San Francisco.' "

That night they saw Austin's two best bands: the Thirteenth Floor Elevators at the Fillmore and the Conqueroo at the Avalon Ballroom.

The next day they went to the Palace of Fine Arts and marveled at its architectural magnificence. There, on its manicured green grass, beside its murky moat, among the grace of its swans and its kaleidoscope of flowers, Li Mam and Michael A. hugged and cuddled like the lovers they had become. Next they rode the Mason Powell cable car to its end and bought flowers from a little old lady street vendor in Union Square. Afterwards they rode the cable car to Fisherman's Wharf. There they went to the Buena Vista Bar for Irish coffee and looked out past Aquatic Park at members of the Dolphin Club in bathing caps swimming in the icy cold bay. They watched old Italian guys play bocce ball. They dined on seafood at Alioto's while being amused by the antics of sea lions on the wharf outside. And, as they walked in the gray-white miasma of fog scudding ashore, enveloping them in its mist, Michael A. just had to say:

"Onward through the fog."

. . .

He told Li Mam he had to get back to Austin for a "gathering of the tribe."

He was on a fatigue high and he knew he was on a fatigue high. He also knew such a mental and physical state left him open to good ideas, so he put himself in an open frame of mind when, on Tuesday evening, July 30, he took the California Flyer to Los Angeles. During his layover in Union Station and before he boarded the Sunset Limited, he placed himself in front of the thirty-foot-tall stained glass window above the entrance. From here he ogled the weirdos, freaks and fairies, dykes and hairies and thought to himself:

I am another like yourselves.

. . .

At the train stop in Tucson Michael A. was astounded by his first ever up close and personal moment with a saguaro cactus and thus it was with immense deference that he sat at its base in the pose of Rodin's The Thinker.

. . .

In El Paso and as he looked over into Mexico, Michael A. ate burritos from the Burrito Lady.

. . .

The Sunset Limited blew into Alpine with all the bluster of the lion in the *Wizard of Oz*. He had last visited Alpine when he had boosted Kilroy's 1966 white Thunderbird and driven Jack to Granpa Gage's funeral. For this particular Alpine stop, though, Michael A. was on foot. He walked the two blocks uphill from the train station to Our Lady of Peace Catholic Church. From there he walked uphill through Baines Park and on up to the rock house he and Jack knew so well. From behind the rock house he walked along the deer trail across 'A' Mountain's north face that was now a wild-flowered field of gold thanks to the monsoon season. The southwest wind was stronger up here on the mountain and so noisy it had a voice of its own, a voice that masked the sound of his approach. Thus, he came right up to and nearly upon a buck mule deer, a ten-pointer. The big guy was on the mountainside laying up for the day and having himself a wild flower Smörgåsbord until Michael A. happened along. For a long moment their eyes met and they knew each other for what they were. Finally Michael A. said.

"Easy, big fella, for I am another like yourself."

He hiked on. Soon he had made a seat for himself on the cross bar of the forty-foot high 'A' of whitewashed rocks that Alpine High

113

students maintained on the mountainside to mark their hometown. As Michael A. had in Tucson with the saguaro cactus, he struck the pose of Rodin's The Thinker. From here he could see for miles and miles through the high desert's clear blue air. To the west was a pair of peaks called the Twin Sisters. To the northwest, toward Fort Davis, he saw the apex of Mitre Peak. Less than a mile away was Hancock Mountain upon whose lower slopes rested the red brick buildings of Sul Ross State University. Seeing the students there, Michael A. thought of the University of Texas and then of his band, of Natasha, of Taj, of Jack and particularly of Jen, how there were no shady oaks for her out here in the high lonesome.

This was when he got the Hill on the Moon idea.

. . .

It was Wednesday evening, July 31. Save for closing the kitchen window, it was time to go, load up the critters, put the basket of wild flowers in the front seat of the Fitty Six and head on down the highway to Austin. Seeing that Jack seemed blue, Jen smiled her perfect smile for him and quoted Granpa Gage:

"Nothin's won if it ain't fun."

Jack grinned and, looking down at the floor, said to Wiley looking up at them, "You ain't nothin' but a hound dog."

His words made Jen grin and, playing along, she looked over at Beep Beep seated in the open kitchen window and said, "How much is that doggie in the window?" She next shooed Beep Beep from the window and, after closing it, said to Jack, "What say next trip out here we put some flower pots in that window so as to keep those goldurned dogs out of it?"

"Sounds like a practical chore of development to me, woman."

"We have made a home of this place, haven't we?"

"I reckon that's why it's called 'the home place'."

With a wink at her man Jen said, "A father works from sun to sun, but a mother's work is never done." She then looked at him with a sly smile until Jack took her meaning and said:

"Well, I'll be, hon—how come ya never tell me nothin' 'til it's a done deal?"

114

Chapter Nine

Back to Austin then. That cultural crossroads which straddles the Balcones Fault as it divides the Texas Hill Country from Her farmland and coastal plain. That gay place that was the 1960s chrysalis and nexus within which thousands of baby boomers were being transformed. Once more to the 19th Street house in which Michael A. aka Marvin was trafficking product via Austin to Boston, Fort Lauderdale, Aspen, the Crown of the Continent and San Francisco. Where Cool Breeze was twirling a toothpick in the corner of his mouth and "recyclin'" and Ma and Mona were downstairs having Tarot readings.

The night of July 31 Jack and Jen, their two dogs and baby chick Boo Boo left behind a living fence, a privy with a view and Mr. Bullsnake. Once Jack climbed in behind the steering wheel of the Fitty Six, Jen scooted over close to him. There Jen paused in disbelief to point at the dashboard where yet another plastic Jesus now hung and say:

"How in the world did Nacho do that?"

Jack just shrugged and started the engine.

On yet another moonlight drive in the cool of the evening the Fitty Six departed Rancho Quien Sabe. In Marathon once again the price of gasoline astounded Jack: "Lawww—fossil fuel's up to 47 cents a throw!" On the road they listened to the Wolfman play the hits: Jr. Walker and the All Stars' "Pucker Up Buttercup", "Sit Down, I Think I love You" by The Mojo Men, "Travelin Man" by Stevie Wonder, "Lady" by Jack Jones plus many others. But what got to Jen most was Aretha Franklin's version of Otis Redding's "Respect."

"I can do that song, Jack, I know I can."

"Yes, ya can, hon, yes, you sure enough can. You can do anything' you set your mind to and you durned sure earned my respect this summer. Thanks to your woman's touch, the home place is livable again."

"Yeah, we did it. It's a home again, isn't it? It's *our* home."

They rode the road to Austin as usual: nothing between them in the cab of the Fitty Six but the couple of inches their hips would not let twin thin waists get to. Meanwhile, in the pickup bed the dogs were snug and safe beneath the upturned *Analuz* and Boo Boo, of course, was in Jen's hair. By not returning via the same route of Juneteenth, they were expanding their horizons by making the trip cyclical: taking the Old El Paso-San Antonio road now known as U.S. Highway 90. They crossed the Great Comanche War Trail that led down into Mexico and headed on east through Sanderson, Del Rio, Brackettville. They drove through Uvalde, Knippa, Sabinal to D'Hanis. At Hondo the Fitty Six turned north on State Highway 173 for the 28 miles to Bandera then turned east onto Highway 46 for the 22 miles to Bulverde. Here they headed north again on U.S. Highway 281 to just before Johnson City where they turned east onto U.S. Highway 290 and on into Austin. On the outskirts of town, as dawn cast out its first light, they renewed their pact:

"We are three, you and me and us. We fight for you, we fight for me, we fight for *us*. We don't live *for* each other, we live *within* each other."

"*Cheep!*"

. . .

It was early in the morning of August 1 and Ma was off with the church ladies on a retreat in Wimberly.

116

Michael A., meanwhile, was sprawled out on the faded red couch in the living room, nekkid as a jaybird beneath a bed sheet because his army green boxer shorts were nowhere to be found. Michael A. was certain that Mona had absconded with his army greens so she could make a voodoo doll of him. Even so, not one of Michael A.'s ungodly ugly toes could keep the beat to Dylan's twenty-plus-minute-tome-of-a-song "Sad Eyed Lady of the Lowlands" as, once again, it was blaring away from the Monkey Ward's Airline Stereo. Though his head hurt and those ungodly ugly toes stunk, Michael A., in his deep nod of drunkenness, believed he was dreaming, dreaming that the licking wetness he felt on his face came from the long slithering wet tongue of a beautiful goddess. Though he could not discern which goddess—Signe, Two Moons, Li Mam or Graciela—he said "Ahhh," in his head and turned said head slightly to one side. Now he began to mull in his slumber the idea of reaching down to his groin to have himself some sex on his own. This shift of mental momentum, however, was when he realized that the beautiful goddess attending to him had not one but two tongues slithering and sloshing his face—and thus in the next heartbeat a daunting fear welled up within Michael A. The Fear got a vice grip on his addled psyche and began to roar through his drunken nothingness to scorch and sear his soul. He was certain that the double wet slobbering on his face was none other than that hellish-heathen-feenie-haint of a Dragon Lady named Mona. The Fear sent a shiver down through his back bone all the way to those now petrified and stinky ungodly ugly toes. It mortified him to think that Mona was basting him with her salty venom and about to swallow him whole, suck him down to become lost forever as part of her evil entrails. A primal urge made him clutch his arms across his chest as if laying himself out for his own funeral. A quiver commenced to tremor through his body and his bloodshot eyes shut themselves even tighter. He felt certain that the end was near for Mona's sloshing sounds were pounding in his ears, raking his brain with pain. He would not go quietly, though; no, that heathen haint would have to struggle to wrench away his last breath. In one

117

unsteady albeit brave motion he grabbed his pillow … but, instead, his quaking hand fell upon something furry and warm and his blurry, bloodshot eyes bulged open to face what he was sure was Oblivion.

However, it was merely two familiar pairs of puppy dog brown eyes.

"Goldurned dawgs," he said to Wiley and Beep Beep. He was reaching for the bed sheet when he heard Jack's voice say:

"Are you jaded? Is the head dead yet? How was the military?"

Secretly overjoyed, Michael A. stood up, the sheet now toga-style about his body, he said with a sneer, "Conscription is another stupid human trick." Then, seeing Jen, he wrapped the sheet tighter and said, "Alas, alack, I fear you find me dishabille."

"We were all very sorry to hear about your dad, Michael A.," Jen said as she set the basket of Rancho Quien Sabe wild flowers on the black-church-door-turned-dining-room-table.

"Thanx, I appreciate the sentiment." Next, the smart aleck in him resurrected, Michael A. said through his smug smile, "Always good to welcome home the cosmic yahoo of the Rio Bravo an' his sweet city Sister Woman what can sing." Spreading his arms wide, he said, "Come on over here'n lay a big'un on me, Jen. Surely we're kissin' cousins by now."

"Not so fast, Mr. Flaws'n Foibles, resident champion of dynamic tension," said Jen. "We have to talk about this fifty kilos of Acapulco Gold from Nacho."

"Oh, that—it's long gone. There's more coming, though, lots. Nacho and Taj and Natasha just sailed up from Cozumel with it."

"*Cheep!*"

. . .

On the afternoon of Thursday, August 1, Jack drove the Fitty Six to the bus station at Fourth and Congress and picked up Taj and Natasha. Both appeared tan and lean after their time on the *Zak Be* and not at all fatigued from their five-day crossing of the Gulf of Mexico.

Jack was utterly elated to hear Taj speak, hear him say "Que tal, y'all."

. . .

Later that afternoon of August 1, Bicycle Annie was standing beside her dilapidated yet still somewhat pink Princess bicycle in the shade of the 19th Street house's garage, burlap bag of recyclables at her feet. Having finished counting her recyclable pay, Annie began to ramble on about the southwest corner of Congress Avenue and Sixth Street, saying:

"That particular lot was bought from the Republic of Texas one hundred and twenty-nine years ago today. On that day, August 1, 1839, the $2800 laid out was the highest price paid for any lot in an auction held to raise money to finance the construction of the State Capitol building. Back then Sixth Street was called Pecan Street and the lot on the southwest corner of Congress Avenue and Pecan Street was considered prime property because Pecan Street was the flattest route into town for wagons. Scarborough's Department Store is there now."

Cool Breeze handed Annie her now empty burlap bag and began to pick his teeth with his toothpick as he said, "Do tell, Miss Annie, do tell. But let's get to what August 1st is now an' that dastardly two years ago today."

"I didn't see nary a mention of it in today's paper," said Bicycle Annie. Then, brightening, she said, "But I did read where Johnny Carson's *Tonight Show* sidekick Ed MacMahon is today's guest star for Aqua Fest."

. . .

It was still Thursday, August 1, two years since Charles Whitman went on his massacre two blocks away atop the University of Texas Tower. In addition to being a memorial rite for that day of loss, tonight's communal dinner at the 19th Street house would be the band's first full reunion since Juneteenth. It was already unique because "Michael A.'s Chili" was being served with "Cool Breeze Greens."

119

Spinning on the turntable of the Monkey Ward's stereo was "Cheap Thrills." Jack and Jen and Taj and Natasha each remarked how much the kittens had grown as the purring Hannah and Hazel, Dot, Persia and Phoebe rubbed up against their legs. Wiley and Beep Beep gave everyone mendicant looks in hopes of table scraps. Michael A., wanting to impress, handed out the red-white-and-blue Aqua Fest skipper pins he had bought for $1 but were worth $9.50 in admissions. Tonight's reunion was a candlelight dinner same as on Juneteenth, this time lit by a solitary votivo made from Jack and Jen's candelilla work down along the Rio Grande. The centerpiece for the black church-door-turned-dining-room-table was Jen's basketful of Big Bend wild flowers. Cool Breeze had set aside his worries about Mona so he and Jen could show off their "business idea", a line of T-shirts called Cool Breeze Teez. He had also brought a mess of his special greens for dinner. At each end of the table was a jar of Yucatecan honey, one of hundreds that had come up on the *Zak Be* along with hundreds of hamacas, chanclas, peasant blouses, guayaberas and tons of pot.

Natasha, in a T-shirt saying *Caution: contents under pressure,* sat at one end of the black church-door-turned-dining-room-table. Taj sat at the other end wearing a T-shirt that said *For a limited time only.* Jen sat next to Natasha and Jack sat next to Jen. Jen's T-shirt said *Now playing* and Jack's said *Supplies are limited.* Opposite Jack sat Michael A. in his *Inspired by an actual event* T-shirt. Next to Michael A. and seated in front of Jen was Cool Breeze in a T-shirt that said *This end up.* In his afro was his star lily, but there was no toothpick in the corner of his mouth.

Each member of the dinner party gave the others a conspiratorial wink as the food was passed around the table and, unlike previous dinners, Taj had something to say:

"Que tal, y'all."

"That's a Spanish greeting with a Texas twist," Natasha said. "Means 'Hello, how's everythin', y'all?'"

"No kiddin'," said Michael A., teasing. "Us Mexamerilebs didn't know that."

"Us Mexican Americans neither," said Jack, also teasing.

"Oh, hush, you two," said Jen.

After dinner Taj and Jack washed and dried the dishes. While Michael A. listened in and Cool Breeze looked on, the band's two city girls gabbed about their summer vacations.

Jen said, "We slept in our hamaca the whole time."

"Us too," Natasha said.

Jen said, "Was it a good sail back?"

Natasha threw up her hands and said, "*Whewww!* A five-day passage is certainly a rite of passage—I definitely came out it stronger."

"Summering in the Big Bend made me stronger too but in a different way," Jen said. "Did you know we got a baby chick? We named her Boo Boo."

"So I hear, Mother Hen Jen," Natasha said, smiling and nodding. Then: "Did Taj tellya we made honey in a hollow log?"

"Uh huh," Jen said then reached over to rub Michael A.'s army buzzcut as she said, "Your fuzzy ol' head sure resembles my little Boo Boo."

Having never been touched so intimately by Jen before, Michael A. blushed. All he could manage to say was, "Awww, I really missed you guys."

"So now we got us a barnyard animal name of Boo Boo," Cool Breeze said. "I seen a black goat the other day—goats is *goood* recyclers."

"Great idea, Cool Breeze," Natasha said. "I was raised on chicken eggs and goat's milk and I believe both are good nutrition."

"They do eat durn near everything," Michael A. said. "We wouldn't have to worry about mowing the grass anymore. But a goat would for sure eat Marvin the scarecrow and I bet there's a good chance it'd raid the garden and eat up your other recycling idea."

Jen said, "What's your other recycling idea, Cool Breeze?"

"An earth worm farm."

"Ouu, cool," Jen said. "They say earth worms make the best growing soil."

Natasha said, "What did you do for Jack's birthday, Jen?"

"Lots," Jack said as he came in from the kitchen to join them.

"One of which, ya big lug" Jen said, playfully punching Jack on the shoulder, "was to bake you a cake in a Dutch oven."

"Down in Cozumel we ate cochinita pibil and pollo pibil made in a pit," Natasha said. "We also dived the Octopus's Garden and saw a sunrise from the bottom of the sea plus we saved a whale shark caught in a fishing net.

"We also saw blue-green lightning," Taj said as he came in from the kitchen.

"We ate tumbleweeds and I learned a little *espanol*," Jen said.

"I learned some *espanol* too," Natasha said. "I even learned some Maya."

Jen said, "Me too—*Bis be'*, baby."

"*Bis be'* to you too, Sis," Natasha said. "I also learned about Maya blue and xutan and The Forces That Are and what 'Maya karma' means, but not 'Maya Karma' with a capital "K." Best of all I learned to dive—now I'm a bubble junkie. Mayaluum transformed me."

"It definitely transformed Taj." Jen said, shaking her head in wonder. "Amazing that he found his voice again."

"Hey, I'm transformed too," Michael A. said, sounding hurt. "I was lost without you guys."

Ignoring him, Natasha said, "It happened when we were 210 feet down. Both Nacho and Taj think it was the seven atmospheres of pressure that fixed his vocal cords."

"I feel certain the exhilaration of the dive itself contributed," Taj said.

"It was an absolutely amazing event," Natasha said. "Taj and I were holding hands when it happened."

"Wow," Michael A. said, his tone serious now. "Kinda sounds like when Jen found her voice in the White Room. Remember?"

Natasha said, nodding. "How well I do—we were all holding hands and harmonizing on 'I Know You Rider' when the candle flickered then went out and zippo bang, our girl Jen could sing like an angel." Then: "Hey, y'all, Taj and I each wrote a couple of songs."

"Me too," Jen said.

"Me too," Jack said.

"We need 'em," said Michael A.

"This band is sooo que tal," Cool Breeze said.

"Forever and always," Taj said.

"Yuck but we sound corny," Natasha said, making a face

Now there was silence save only for collective purring of the kittens who had retired to the faded red couch.

"Goldurned kittens," Michael A. said.

Which was when Wiley licked himself and Beep Beep scratched at a pesky ear itch and Jack said, "Goldurned dawgs."

Which was when in their fish bowl above the Stromberg Carlson television set in-the-floor-to-ceiling bookcase, Thelma and Barney Lou, seemed to grin.

. . .

That night when The Psychedelic Crabs went downstairs to the White Room to practice, they discovered that Michael A.'s mom had returned from her outing with the church ladies. To Michael A.'s surprise and consternation, Ma had her Tarot cards laid out before her.

"From the church ladies to the Tarot cards—that's quite a segue, Ma," Michael A. said. "Actually, it's downright absurd juxtaposition." When Ma began doing a reading for someone no one could see, Michael A. freaked out. "Oh god oh god oh god," he said. "It's gotta be Mona."

"No, it is for our Rain Shadow," Ma said. "She who is the voice by the fire."

"You mother is pals with a basilisk," Taj said.

"I think it's sweet," Jen said.

"Yeah, Mrs. Medina fits right in," Natasha said, smiling her own sly smile.

Then they all looked at Jack holding up the six-figurine terracotta statuette that Nacho had given to the band, the votivo that Jack had left there after the Juneteenth dinner and had jokingly asked Mona to keep lit.

"Cool of you to light the candle, Jack," Natasha said.

"Tonight Jack is our Keeper of the Flame," Taj said, nodding approvingly.

"It wasn't me," Jack said, shaking his head. "I didn't light it and I don't think it was Aunt Sofi because ..."

"Ma won't go near fire," Michael A. said, his face turning pale. "Oh god oh god oh god, it was ..."

"The haint," Cool Breeze said, his eyes wide in fearful amazement.

"Good ol' Mona," Natasha said, smiling and nodding.

"Que tal, Mona," Taj, said, also smiling.

"Ain't it great to be home?" Jen said.

. . .

On Friday, August 2, the morning paper had a small story about an American Leatherneck missing since 1965 who had been killed by Marines as he led a force of Viet Cong. After Jack and Michael A. read this story twice, very carefully each time, Jack said:

"What in the world do you make of that?"

Michael A. thought a bit then shrugged and said, "Caca pasa, chachalaca."

. . .

That same morning, Friday, August 2, Jen was patting the burgundy Triumph 650 motorcycle affectionately with her hand and saying to Michael A., "We got a deal for this consarned contraption?"

Michael A.'s response was to look at Jack who, after a shrug of resignation, said, "Nobody tells me nothin' 'til it's a done deal."

Michael A. now looked at Jen and said, "Okay, Sister Woman, you're on—we got a deal."

This was when Cool Breeze, standing by his 1956 pink Cadillac, had to smile. He smiled even more when Jen paid Michael A. cash for the burgundy Triumph 650 then mounted it and kick-started it to life. Next he grinned with delight as Jen roared out of the driveway onto University and headed for 19th Street.

Cool Breeze dearly liked the sight of an empowered woman.

Before that night's band practice a house meeting was held. The meeting was called after Ma had read the Tarot cards with Jen and Natasha. As a result of that reading and because all of the band-mates felt transformed, it was decided that the band needed a new name. The guys were the first to be okay with it.

"Fine with me," Michael A. said. "Psychedelic Crabs and Purple People Eaters do sorta clash."

"Clearly, it is absurd juxtaposition," Taj said.

"Yeah, when ya think about it," Jack said, "The Pyschedelic Crabs really *is* kind of a corny name even for a rock band."

Jen said, "So how about we call ourselves White Rain?"

Natasha said, "How about The Freedom Fighters?"

"Kaboom," Michael A. said. "Yeah, Kaboom … or Rain Shadow … or The Psychedelic Pharts … or Xutan … or The Austintacious."

"Blue Moon's my choice," Jack said.

"Let us be Que Tal," Taj said. "I believe that would be a good name."

And thus in that moment the band, too, was transformed, taking as their new name the words which Taj had used to break his silence.

That night the band now called Que Tal reworked an on-again-off-again bluesy instrumental where they just "felt one another." They even changed the song's name from "Crab Jam" to "To Success, To Crime: Mum's the Word."

. . .

Jen's old pal from Fort Worth, Jolinda Biggs, dropped by the next day with what in a previous life had been Jen's Pentax 35 mm camera. Jolinda took promotional photos of Que Tal and everybody agreed that the best photo was the one where the band, with Wiley and Beep Beep flanking Jen, was seated one behind the other on the front porch steps.

It was expected by the women present—Jen, Natasha, Jolinda— that Jolinda would be harassed by Que Tal's Male Chauvinsist Pig, the bass player, the Mexamerileb, Michael Antonio Medina. Jen had her death glare ready same as Natasha had ready her new favorite moniker for Michael A.—"self-involved-self-indulgent-spitbird-crab-boy." But Michael A. was a perfect gentleman. Not even one of his utterances referred to Jolinda's abundant bosom. A curious Jen later said to Jack:

"So what's up with Mr. Dynamic Tension, our impish-stinker-hipster-doofus-jiveass-creepy-womanizer of a twisted satyr who demeans women and irks the crap out of me?"

"He's into maintaining good karma right now," Jack said. "He feels that, same as when we launched the band and Purple People Eater, we're embarking on another transforming experience and that we're crossing the threshold into another chrysalis—an' he don't wanta queer the deal."

"A chrysalis is what we are," Jen said, nodding. "A stage of being, or protected growth—yep, that's us."

Jack then said, "Are you saying you now like Michael A.?"

"Little bit." Wincing. "He *cannn* play the dickens out of that Fender bass … and he's a good singer."

"But you still can't bring yourself to love him, canya?"

"Not much." Biting her lower lip. "I'd still bet that as a kid he not only picked his nose but that he ate his boogers too." Then, hands on her hips: "An' phooey on your ol' 'he's into maintaining good karma right now', Ben Jack Gage, 'cause your sneaky cousin's just trying to impress Natasha in hopes of getting her back."

"Well, yeah, that too … I love him dearly but, oh, how well I know him."

"Wanta know a secret?" Jen said with a mischievous look on hers face.

"Always."

"Welll, Jolinda got kicked out of the Nu Mus on accounta she's—" Then leaned over and whispered in Jack's ear, causing him to draw back in surprise.

"*Nawww!*"

"Yep." Nodding emphatically. "Canya believe it?"

Jack said, "Well, it certainly has been known to happen—not that there's anything wrong with it." Then he paused before saying, "Just what's behind that Tarzan yell Natasha's been doing every morning since we all came back home?"

"You mean 'Prague today! Chicago tomorrow!'" Giving it some oomph.

"Right. Okay, I know about Prague—Prague Spring an' all like that—but what's she so all-fired hep on Chicago for?"

"We need to talk," Jen said.

. . .

Somewhere in the middle of that same night Taj and Michael A. crossed paths on the way to the bathroom. It was the first time they had been alone together since Taj and Natasha had become a couple and it could have been an awkward encounter. But as they passed each other Michael A. not breaking stride, not giving it much, said:

"Que tal, y'all?"

Next Taj, not breaking stride, either, answered by saying, "I am good. I am home with my own. I am happy."

"Yeah, me too," Michael A. said and walked on by.

. . .

At the next night's dinner—Jen's Vegetarian Chili—Taj put through House Rules Numbers Seven through Thirteen.

Number Seven: No sentences between housemates beginning with "You never."

Number Eight: No sentences between housemates beginning with "You always."

Number Nine: No sentences between housemates beginning with "Are you sure?"

Number Ten: No sentences between housemates beginning with "Don't."

Number Eleven: No sentences between housemates beginning with "I *told* you."

Number Twelve: No sentences between housemates beginning with "You made me."

Number Thirteen: No sentences between housemates beginning with "You need to."

After each of these rules was passed, Michael A. kept giving Natasha his sly smile until she caved in and said, "I take some getting used to, okay?"

"Tell me about it," Michael A. said. "That's partly why I gave you Fromm's *The Art of Loving.*" Then he looked at Taj and, trying to sound sincere, said, "Believe me, Taj, I wish I had what you got 'cause you got what it takes."

Jack then proposed House Rule Number Fourteen: No sentences between housemates beginning with "We need to talk."

It failed to pass, three to two, only Jack and Michael A. voting for it.

Michael A. next brought up his Hill on the Moon idea and it passed unanimously. Michael A., Jack and Taj then used Michael A.'s printing press to crank out the hand bills.

The next day Bicycle Annie and the street person Ryder tacked up those hand bills all around the University.

. . .

The front page news on Wednesday, August 7, was that Nixon was all set to get it.

But that was already old news.

. . .

Those in Que Tal would always say that it was the xutan of their Hill on the Moon Love-In that let the music take over that Wednesday night at practice. They believed this transformation came to pass because Que Tal was under the gun since the band had so little time to get their act together for their Hill on the Moon Love-In. And indeed it did come to pass that, on Wednesday night, August 7, while harmonizing on "Little Bitty Pretty One" that the chrysalis known as Que Tal took on a life of its own.

"Bands aren't made—they're born," Michael A. would always say about that night.

"Most people," Jack said, "go to their graves with their music still within them—but not us. No way."

"Our music is alive," Jen said.

"It thrives," said Natasha.

"Our music *is*," said Taj.

"Weird, wild stuff," said Cool Breeze. "I dig it."

When it happened, Michael A. stubbed his toe, Natasha pitched a bitch, Jen gasped then fainted dead away into Jack's arms and Taj saw The Forces That Are right before his eyes as he *sang* and held back his drum beat just enough for Que Tal to mesh and meld. But nobody noticed Ma dancing in the corner. Nor that Wiley and Beep Beep chased a ghostly albino squirrel up their favorite shady oak tree on University Avenue.

Or that Thelma and Barney Lou got it on.

That sultry summer night it was 88 degrees when it happened in the White Room of the two story red brick house at 200 West 19th Street. While Que Tal was harmonizing on "Little Bitty Pretty One" the band joined to become spiritually whole. They became one entity musically, an entity that danced with one arm swinging free, danced like grains of sand on their way to the sea. They interpreted the rhythm of life as body talk … and they saw a new *her* there on the south wall of the White Room. The band collectively witnessed an apparition, a new being there beside Ma trying to feign itself as a vague shadow dancing in the corner. This new being, this personage in the form of a dancing shadow was white as rain and doing the Watusi, undulating within the black curtain glowing in the black light.

The band now called Que Tal believed this Tiny Dancer personage, this new being in the White Room, was their soul companion, their uay.

And thus it came to be that from then on Que Tal's rhythm was one and this one force was all.

Que Tal had *IT*.

When Nacho was told, his only words were "Maya Karma."

. . .

On Thursday, August 8, Radio KNOW was saying that at the Republican National Convention in Miami Beach Richard Milhaus Nixon had been nominated on the first ballot to run for president of the United States of America. Bicycle Annie, however, after dropping her burlap recycling bag at Cool Breeze's feet was saying:

"Town Lake was only a couple of years old when the city fathers came up with Aqua Fest back in 1962 so as to plug Austin and its surrounding lakes as a vacation spot. The first one started off on August 3, 1962, and went on 'til the 12th of that month. That Art Linkletter feller was the headliner."

"Kids say the darndest things," Cool Breeze said.

"There was a 150 mile canoe race," Bicycle Annie said, "and a fishing tournament, a sailing regatta and a night time parade on Town Lake plus a military parade, concerts, golf tournament, dances, rodeo, fireworks—the whole shebang."

"Yes'um" Cool Breeze said. "I recall them fireworks, I surely do."

Bicycle Annie said, "In 1964 they called it Rio Noche on account of the water parade."

"Yes'um," Cool breeze said. "These days the parade makes for a whole lot of traffic congestion down there in the Latino part of town but since these folks got no clout, that's the way it is ... for now anyhow 'cause the times is a-changin'." Then, almost winsome: "Nice parade though, at night'n all ... wish I could be cool enough ta just float along'n be parta somethin' like dat."

. . .

On Thursday morning, August 8, it was not a long, somber drive south from 19th and University to St. Austin's Catholic Church at 2010 Guadalupe. The band got there with bells on, literally: at 7 a.m. because they had been up all night practicing and still celebrating the arrival of their uay and Taj's cow bell could be heard up and down 19th Street. That morning's memorial service for Captain

Medina was conducted with full military honors. Michael A. and Jack had to stand beside Widow Medina and hold the grief-stricken Ma up by the elbows. Scooter Culero sent flowers from Vietnam. Jen sang "Row Me Over to the Other Side, Dad." The Austinites who showed up said, "He was one of ours." The folded flag the honor guard guy presented Ma would later hang beside the other United States flag over the faded red couch back at 19th and University.

Michael A. addressed the gathering. He said stuff such as "Bravery is but a moment in the morning sun before the day is done." He told them Walks in Blue Green's tale of how his dad bought it at the hands of the bushwhacking Charlie sniper. He said, "More than anything, my dad was a military man. He was also a man I knew, someone I used to listen to. Some of what he told me I recall: life is too short, life is for the living, life is but a brief victory over that what's gonna get ya … and, oh yeah, 'Lordy, lordy, look at the spread on that one.'" Michael A. continued by saying, "The last thing my father said to me before going off to Nam was 'The future is murder.' He also said other things too like 'It's all relative' and 'Parenting is the least developed skill.' And, oh yeah, my all-time personal favorite: 'Caca pasa, chachalaca.'"

Later, after the ceremony, as they all stood on the church steps, Cool Breeze removed the star lily in his afro and, handing it to the widow, said:

"That was a nice sendoff, ma'am, an' I surely do appreciate a nice sendoff."

. . .

That same day all of Que Tal crossed 19th Street and went up the steps to the front porch of Gamma Sigma fraternity house. There on the porch Michael A., representing Que Tal, negotiated a Gamma Sig gig with chief frat rat Kilroy for Wednesday, August 21. Que Tal was to get a $500 payoff. Even better, Jack and Jen and Taj and Natasha and Michael A. had all gotten a special feeling while standing on the steps of the Gamma Sig house and looking north across the street at 200 West 19th Street.

Each band member was awed that they actually lived in such a cool place.

Also, Taj noted for the first time a second red brick chimney on the roof of the 19th Street house. It was on the west wall.

Chapter Ten

Natasha would come to see that Thursday afternoon of August 8, as another calamity of events. But, unlike that other calamity of events that day on the beach down in Mayaluum, the Hill on the Moon Love-In was a culture clash: two factions of Human Nature rubbing up against one another … and the ripple effect was violence.

Michael A. had always liked the name Hill on the Moon. The Bonds lived there and Crady Bonds had named the acreage off City Park Road Hill on the Moon while on an acid trip. Good people lived there. A freewheeling, freebooting bunch, some of whom came from New York, some from California in a band called Wildfire. Ensconced within their property was a hillside with a flat clearing that was a natural amphitheater. Because the Hill on the Mooners liked to party, they had erected an outdoor stage in the clearing's center. They had also put in a public address system plus all the electronic gear a rock and roll band needed.

Michael A. liked to party, too, but his principal aim for the Hill on the Moon Love-In was to launder money. "The show must go on" was his anthem in the days leading up to Que Tal's first gig.

"On to Chicago" was Natasha's anthem.

"Ever forward" was Jen's.

"Que tal, y'all" was Taj's.

"Dogs run free" was Jack's.

"We cool" was Cool Breeze's.

Nacho was noticeably absent. He would have been needed.

Que Tal decked themselves out for the Love-In. They went native—Native American. They drove the Fitty Six down into the Hill on the Moon sporting Piegan Blackfeet elkskin moccasins, war shirts brightly beaded across the chest with buckskin fringe along the sleeves. They carried dance sticks, a walking stick, a flute carved out of a river reed, a deer horn whistle, a tomahawk pipe. Jack wore his peregrine falcon feather in his braided hair and Michael A. carried his handwoven, beaded elkskin medicine bag. Cool Breeze wore not one but two star lilies in his afro.

Que Tal was tuning up to start off their set with "Summertime" when it happened. But maybe it should have been "Summertime Blues" for the Hill on Moon Love-In turned out to be that rare Purple People Eater Production whose memory forever burned a wound into the collective soul of the band. It left behind an image that would sear a deep scar.

It was flat out no good horrible what happened there that Thursday afternoon, August 8, 1968.

. . .

The crowd was chanting "Parrrteee parrrteee parrrteee."

"Dogs run free," was all Jack could ever recall saying at the gig. Jack had said this because dogs cannot abide loud music and so when Que Tal started tuning up, Wiley and Beep Beep and the other dogs present ran as a pack up to the ridge atop the hillside. It just so happened that the dogs headed for the ridge just as a gathering of law enforcement officers and hangers-on on the other side were in the midst of imbibing around a keg. Offended because Que Tal's instrument tune up had already begun to drown out their own music, about twenty of this bunch—two of them with shotguns, all of them in gray Stetsons like Granpa Gage had worn in his ranger-ing days—marched off toward the Hill on the Moon. They marched as would a lynch mob determined to set things right.

Meanwhile, onstage Michael A. was saying to Taj, "Darn good gig for money laundering."

134

"There must be three hundred people here," Taj said.

"Let's call it a thousand … or whatever the tax man will allow."

Nearby, Natasha held her flute carved out of a river reed and Jen held a deer horn whistle. Both bandmates were already *seeing* "Summertime" even before it began: closing their eyes, feeling it, being harmonious to the bone, loving its lightning in their soul. They did not hear their two dogs commence to keen at atop the ridge, send forth an eerie wail from deep within them, lower their heads to bray some more then move forward with interest as dogs will do.

But Jen and Natasha did hear the shotgun blasts that destroyed two lives.

Two dogs died. Two loved ones were lost to violence.

Natasha could only lower her head in prayer.

Jen, as though she were beseeching some higher authority for an answer, fell down to her left knee and spread her arms. Her eyes took on a look of hysteria as she craned her head toward the sky and her mouth went agape with a horror that gripped her so hard it wrung from her a scream.

It was a primal scream.

. . .

Violence will always end a Love-In.

Jack and Jen took their murdered dogs away in the Fitty Six and laid Wiley and Beep Beep to rest just as they had been in life: side by side. They were buried at the foot of their favorite shady oak alongside University Avenue, the one nearest their bedroom window, the one they liked to pee on. The funeral was witnessed by Taj and Natasha, Cool Breeze, Bicycle Annie, the street person Ryder and Michael A., of course, who bought flowers from Connelly's Florist to be laid on the graves. All were speechless save Jack who said:

"Dogs run free."

Shock ruled until bitterness set in.

Bitterness set in that night as Jen brushed her hair in her and Jack's bedroom. Jack was on the waterbed watching her when her

135

sullenness seethed up from within her and began to vent, when she said in the most listless voice Jack had heard from her since the murder of Robert F. Kennedy two months before:

"I'm not going to cry, I won't shed a tear … I'm going to Chicago with Natasha and Taj."

"I know," Jack said, trying to gentle her, "you told me, remember?" Then he sighed and, trying to reason with her, analyze her feelings, said, "You've been radicalized by this tragedy, Jen. Wiley and Beep Beep lost their lives and it's radicalized you."

"Actually it began when my parents died. That was when I learned the difference between 'here' and 'gone' and that part of life is scabs and scars and healing with feeling." Then, her voice almost a growl: "Be here now!" Next: "And 'lost their lives' is a meaningless term, Jack. They *kill*ed our dogs! *They killed our dogs!*"

"You're right. They murdered Wiley and Beep Beep."

"And by murdering Wiley and Beep Beep those creeps with guns and grins and hats and boots put hate in my heart." She let her pain ache a moment before she said, "It's gonna be a new dawn in Chicago, Jack. Like Martin Luther King said 'There is the fierce urgency of now.'"

Jack now began to ramble, too, saying "Yeah, yeah, and I don't pick the sunset nor do I get to choose the sunrise—caca pasa, chachalaca, life is compromise, life is timing." His voice rising, he said, "It's just that I feel in my gut that I should shield you, Jen, you know, protect you from pain an' suffering. Lawsy mercy, you're going on a long road trip an' that makes me think of how I lost my folks in a highway accident and, well, hey, you'n me are both orphans—an' I don't wanta be no orphaned lover. We're just two more stubborn souls, the jack and the jenny of jackasses." He paused before saying, "Awww hell, hon, it ain't my fault that part of love is worryin' about your lover."

"I worry about you too," Jen said, meaning it. "Like, for instance, that you'll eat right while I'm gone, that you'll stay up all night playing your guitar down in the White Room."

Jack shrugged. "You know me—food's just fuel ... an' Aunt Sofi'll see to it me'n Cuz eat right ... an' if I feel inspired, well, that's okay for a lonely guy."

"Aunt Sofi's leaving today for two weeks, Jack. She's going to Disneyland with a bunch of church ladies—did you know that?"

Jack sighed and said, "Nobody tells me nothin' 'til it's a done deal."

. . .

Bitterness did not set in for Michael A. By evening he had rolled with Life's Hill on the Moon punch and had come up swinging.

After the funeral, he rode off on the Triumph 650. He went down 19th Street and took a right turn. For eleven blocks he rode south on Red River. He was on his way to the cop shop at 8th and Interstate 35. Once there he was going to tell the law what some of their own had done at the Hill on the Moon Love-In, see what they would do about it, find out if there was any justice in this town.

But by the time he had come to the stop light at 8th and Red River, he had realized the Hill on the Moon was in the Travis County Sheriff's jurisdiction. Now Michael A. found himself looking long and hard to his left, at 801 Red River. Long and hard enough that he became so remarkably clear of mind that he blew off going to the law.

That long and hard look at 801 Red River put Michael A.—and the band—through some changes.

For it was a life-changing look.

. . .

After the dogs' funeral, Cool Breeze told Jen he thought it had been a nice sendoff—only to have Jen look Cool Breeze straight in the eye and tell him he did not look so good. As he walked away from this exchange, Cool Breeze was saying to himself:

"Ah don't need nooo woman to gut my nuts—ah ain't gonna be like my daddy an' die already dead inside. Life is for the living."

137

Jen's comment had hit a nerve because of what Cool Breeze called "The Nam." The way he saw it those long months were not his finest moments. His lieutenant, a lifer and veteran of the Korean War, was not gung ho. The man saw through the bull that was The Nam and was not going to lose his life to a fragmentary grenade tossed into his tent at night by one of his own men. So he had led his recon patrols only a short distance away from the platoon where, for a day or two, the patrol would hang out and smoke dope then return to the platoon, report they had seen no sign of Charlie. Between patrols was routine tedium: the soldiers did little jobs and relaxed. They barbequed steaks taken from the Special Forces guys' air-conditioned bunkers. They barbequed these steaks in a 55-gallon drums cut in half with blow torches. The other half of the drum was used for long soaks, their version of Roman baths.

The drums had previously contained Agent Orange.

Later, Cool Breeze and others had wondered if their aching joints were due to Agent Orange. But the doctors at the Veterans Administration hospital in Waco said, "Nah, no way, take some of these pills and go back home."

"War," Cool Breeze liked to say. "What's it good for? Nothin' but destruction and … death."

That night, the night of the day Wiley and Beep Beep were murdered, Cool Breeze took sick.

. . .

On Friday morning, August 9, Michael A. found Cool Breeze in his 1956 pink Caddy. On his chest was a star lily.

He was asleep forever.

Almost immediately the street person called Ryder came out from the shadows and Bicycle Annie rode up on her still somewhat pink Princess bicycle.

Michael A., Ryder and Bicycle Annie talked and decided what to do.

. . .

Jack awoke to see it was Jen. His eyes were still full of sleep but right away he was saying to her in an unsteady voice, "Darlin', last night was the greatest, most profound sentient experience of my young life. Hon, I never—"

This was when Jen put a finger to his lips and said, "Hush." As she began stroking her man's forehead, she said, "I have to tell you about Cool Breeze."

. . .

Michael A. made all the arrangements. First he got the go-ahead from Cool Breeze's momma and granmomma. Jackson Lamar Brown, aka Cool Breeze, the Vietnam vet who recycled before most knew what that was, who replaced the toothpick in his mouth with a star lily in his afro, who called Michael A. "Mister Hoochie Coochie Man," who conducted business out of a pink 1956 Cadillac was going to get his last wish: a big sendoff.

It happened at 9 p.m. on Friday night, August 9, during Aqua Fest's Rio Noche Water Parade on Town Lake. Michael A. used his printing press to come up with the proper parade documents so Cool Breeze could ride in the last float, a dozen star lilies from Connelly's Florist on his chest. Away Jackson Lamar Brown went in *Analuz*, Michael A. and Jack paddling him downstream before 150,000 folks looking on from Festival Beach, many of those folks East Austinites saying goodbye to "one of our own."

"We cool," Granmomma said as *Analuz* drifted by.

"We celebrating a life," said Momma as the float that cradled her son passed by.

It seemed fitting that, being the last float, it set off a thirty-minute shower of color courtesy of Jack's Fireworks.

"A fete accompli," Michael A. said, "for a man I knew, someone I used to talk to."

"Life is but a brief victory over what's gonna get you," Jack said.

Later the ashes of Lamar Jackson Brown would be cast into the briny deep, there to be consumed by sea life then discharged and eaten and discharged ad infinitum.

139

"Recyclin'" forever and ever.

. . .

On Tuesday, August 20, 1968, Prague Spring was crushed beneath
the boots of 200,000 Warsaw Pact troops. With this invasion began
a period of enforced and oppressive "normalization."

That night Natasha was silent at dinner but particularly brilliant
on her organ and harmonica during band practice.

. . .

Jen decided to keep the scream from the Hill on the Moon Love-In.
It was cathartic, it purged her demons. Strangely enough, the scream
became Que Tal's signature after the Gamma Sig gig on Wednesday,
August 21.

It was a rare fraternity party indeed for 1968 because neither
"Louie Louie" nor "Land of a Thousand Dances" was played. Que
Tal both felt and played in fine fettle. With the band's new material
Que Tal had expanded its repertoire to more than twenty songs. In-
spired by their summer vacations, the band members had worked up
"Dawn Song" and "Maya Blue" by Natasha, "Closure" and "Bridge
Beyond the Light" by Taj, "Cruisin for Burgers" and "Streaks" by
Michael A., "Planesence" and "Draggin'n Driftin' " by Jack, and
"White Rain", "Dancing Lightning" and "Pagan Pachanga" by Jen.

And, of course, Jen wowed all with her voice on Aretha's "Respect" and "(You Make Me Feel Like) A Natural Woman."

The band's closer—"To Success, To Crime: Mum's the Word"—
actually had the Sigs down on the floor doing the Alligator.

"You guys *got it*—we wantya for more gigs, maybe even as our
house band," Kilroy said. "And that Jen, man, that girl can sing—
that scream of hers is as chilling as a rebel yell."

Later, the band came to see Jen's rebel yell as symbolic of the
summer of '68. The deaths of Captain Medina and of Wiley and
Beep and Cool Breeze and the violence unleashed later that month
during the Democratic National Convention in Chicago all made

for a ball of emotion, a wad of rage that stuck in their communal craw and had to be vented lest it fester and poison their idealism.

. . .

It was after the Gamma Sig gig, Thursday morning, 3 a.m. and Taj and Jack and Michael A. were hauling band equipment out the front door of the Gamma Sig house so they could load it into the Fitty Six. It was a nearby Gamma Sig who pointed at the 19th Street house and said:

"Cool house you guys got, especially the way the UT Tower shows over the top of the roof."

When Taj paused to look at the Tower, at its top visible above the roofline of the 19th Street house, something else caught his eye: a muted glow atop the red chimney. Taj then heard Jack say:

"Well, I'll be goldurned. She's just sitting up there pretty as can be, ain't she?"

"Oh god oh god oh god," Michael A. said.

Taj said nothing. He was just glad that Mona was coming out of her shell.

Chapter Eleven

The full moon had just set in the west and first light was visible through the shady oak trees on University Avenue. It was Friday, August 23, and out back of the 19th Street house it was 68 degrees. None of the five members of Que Tal present was teary-eyed. There was no blubbering nor bawling now that it was time to say goodbye. Though Cool Breeze's last gift to them had been the just-released Fleetwood Mac's "Mr. Wonderful," the music from the Fitty Six's just-installed eight track stereo was The Jefferson Airplane's "And I Like It."

Michael A. was leaning against the driver's door of the 1956 pink Cadillac. He wore nothing but cutoffs and his rose colored glasses. His arms were folded across his chest and his legs were crossed at the ankles—hanging back because he figured he had few if any lines in the scene about to unfold.

Jen stood beside her newly purchased burgundy Triumph 650 motorcycle –her ride to Chicago. She had on cutoffs, too, and a white T-shirt whose front said *Use no hooks.* On her feet were combat boots.

Natasha stood next to her brand new black Honda 450. She also wore cutoffs and her white T-shirt read *Caution: contents under pressure.* Over her heart was Michael A.'s round white stickpin that said *Don't trust anyone over thirty.* Her long hair was in a ponytail and over her shoulder was Michael A.'s handwoven, beaded elkskin medicine bag. A *Seeya in Chicago* sticker was on the bag and a copy of *The Rag* and *The Rose in the Gun* protruded from it. Stooping to lace up her combat boots, she said:

"Man, it's like la maya say—you really do feel events before they happen."

"It is most definitely xutan," Taj said with a nod. Taj also wore cutoffs and combat boots and his white T-shirt said *Fun for all ages!* He stood beside his brand new black Kawasaki 450 holding today's newspaper. Strapped behind the Kawasaki's seat was Natasha's army green medic's bag. In the Maya rucksack on his back were the papers for the $30 billion lawsuit against the government of the United States he would file in Chicago on behalf of the bees and hummingbirds for compensation owed due to all the work they did to keep the country going.

"This moment feels like graduation," Jack said. "Know whut I mean? The best of times and the worst of times."

"I guess that's what pregnancy feels like too," Jen said, shouldering her own Maya rucksack to reach into her long hair and extract Boo Boo. Next she looked at Jack beside her. He was in his James Dean pose of thumbs hooked in the front pockets of his cutoffs. In his braided hair was a yellow rose courtesy of Connelly's Florist. Exchanging the yellow rose for Boo Boo, Jen said, "Are you blue, Cowboy?"

"Nawww." Not giving it much.

"Cheep!"

"Are you sure?"

Michael A., not giving it much, either, said, "House Rule Number Eight states there shall be no sentences beginning with 'Are you sure'."

"Well, he *does* look worried," Jen said, hands now on her hips. "Ben Jack Gage, are you trying to pull the rug out from beneath us freedom fighters?"

"No, ma'am, no rug pullin' here." Then Jack leaned forward and bussed her on the nose. "I'm your longtime man. I love you, you love me, we love each other, 'Us' is bigger than both of us. Though you smile like a child, you're always a woman to me."

"You're on," Jen said. "Friends until the end. Forever here. Here forever." Then she thumped herself once on her heart with her fist. "Ever forward," she said and kissed him full on the lips.

"House Rule Number Six," Michael A. said, again not giving it much. "'No public displays of affection.'"

Jack leaned close to Jen and said, his voice a whisper, "No helmet, hon?"

"Girls ride free." Also whispering.

"Cheep!"

Still whispering, Jack said, "Do you still love me?"

"Forever and ever."

Grinning with pride now, Jack pretended to notice Jen's combat boots for the first time. No longer whispering, he said, "You goin' to war, girl?"

"Well, I *am* a freedom fighter," she said, sapphire eyes sparkling as she began to put her hair up in a ponytail.

"Jen and I are on the National Mobilization Committee to End the War in Vietnam," Natasha said, "and Taj is a member of the Youth International Party."

"That is correct," Taj said, "I am a Yippie." Then he proceeded to wad up the front page of the newspaper he had been holding. Next he leaned against his motorcycle seat and began patting out a familiar beat with his right foot, countering it with downbeats from his left foot while squeezing the ball of wadded-up front page like an accordion to produce a marimba-like sound.

"'I Feel Free' a la our pleasant presence, our Everyman," Michael A. said.

Everybody got into it then, all them humming along before harmonizing the chorus. When done, Jen said:

"Okay, we know we rock ... now let's roll."

"Cheep!"

. . .

145

For the two bandmates left behind it was a week of worry, waiting and watching.

Over the weekend they went to movies and beer joints and sought out air-conditioning all over Austin. They cruised for burgers in the pink Caddy. They plotted drifting wood and daydreamed of making bubbles in the Caribbean Sea. They shot pool. They used their passes at Barton Springs. Mostly, they did little and they felt like doing less. They were uninspired. They considered weeding the garden on the west side of the house—but did no more than look at the garden with long, glum faces.

"'Tis an unweeded garden that grows to seed'," Jack said.

"Hamlet, Act I, Scene 2," Michael A. said, looking at the tuxedo clad Marvin the Martian scarecrow. "There ain't no kaboom nowhere around here."

For Sunday, August 25, the eve of the convention in Chicago, Austin's high temperature was 92 degrees at 6 P.M. By 8 P.M. it had dropped to 91. The cousins had just finished peeing off the east end of the front porch. Jack plopped down in Granpa Gage's Bentwood rocker and Michael A. settled himself into a purple butterfly chair. In the living room the Monkey Ward's Stereo had on Radio KNOW's Jay Jackson playing Sly and the Family Stone's "Dance to the Music." Both cousins wore only boxer shorts, Jack in black Fruit of the Loons, Michael A. his army green ones—he had found them behind the White Room's black curtain. It was Michael A. who barely raised his beer can to say, his tone nearly inaudible:

"Here's to House Rule Number Three."

"'Underwear for men required'," Jack said, barely raising his beer.

"If it weren't for Rule Number Three," Michael A. said, "we'd probably be out here on the porch in fronta God'n everbody bareass buck nekkid."

"Gotta have law'n order," Jack said and sipped from his can of seventy-nine-cents-a-six-pack of Milwaukee's Best. After wiping his mouth, he looked down at the can and said, "Ain't exactly the champagne of bottled beers, is it, Cuz?"

"'Better living through chemistry' as Dupont says," Michael A. said then took a sip of his own brew.

"As Ronnie Raygun used to say for General Electric, 'Progress is our most important product.'"

"Mota will getcha through times of no money better than money'll getcha through times of no mota."

. . .

Come Monday, August 26, the routine dissolved into an even more desultory scene. Jack could not watch and Michael A. would not watch, so all network coverage of the Democratic National Convention at the 19th Street house was put on hiatus. Jack and Michael A. elected to get their Chicago updates from the newspaper and radio because each was a "hot medium" for information and did not involve the high sensory involvement of television. That fateful week Cousin Ben Jack of Rancho Quien Sabe down along the Rio Grande would get up as soon as he heard the thump of the newspaper hitting the front porch. He would then go outside in his blue Fruit of the Loons and Lucchese boots with Boo Boo in tow and pick up the paper. Next he would pee off the east end of the porch then go over to Granpa Gage's bentwood rocker to sit down for his daily dose of despair.

At some point Cousin Michael A. would show up in his army green boxer shorts. He would toss out a handful of chicken scratch for Boo Boo to work on and nod a lethargic hello at the five kittens seemingly always nearby. Next he would adjust his rose colored glasses and plop down in a purple butterfly chair. There he would scratch his crotch, pick up the newspaper left for him by Cousin Jack in the adjacent butterfly and say to it:

"Mawnin,' blues—blues, how do you do?"

That wild and whacky week Cowboy Blue and The Hoochie Coochie Man alternated between seething with rage or being wracked with worry about their loved ones in Chicago—or else they were flat out disgusted with the Powers That Be … or ashamed of themselves for not having gone to Chicago.

147

"Well, at least we who sit and wait still serve," Michael A. said.

"Bulll," Jack said. "Now serve up another one just like the other one."

. . .

That Monday, August 26, they read in the newspaper that the night before over two thousand hippies yelling "pig" had clashed with one hundred cops in Lincoln Park. According to the article, "pig" was the hippie word for "cop."

They read that Six thousand federal troops would back up eighteen thousand National Guard troops in Chicago.

From "Hints from Heloise" they learned how to wash a chamois by using mild soap, cold water, a cold water rinse then stretch and dry the chamois in a cool place.

Wick Fowler's Fowler Fare said divers did indeed find the dollar LBJ tried to throw across the Pedernales River.

The Mexican government said it would offer concessions to dissident students so as to make for a smooth operation of the Olympic Games slated for October 22-27.

American doctors were performing undercover abortions on the basis of fetal chromosome tests that indicated the coming birth of a mongoloid idiot.

Texas led the United States in murders with 1059, 293 in Houston alone.

In Chicago a peaceful circle of folks had sung the national anthem and "America the Beautiful." Also a bus strike was crippling an already lame system.

Twice as many Americans favored former vice president Richard M. Nixon according to the Gallup poll because most thought Nixon would do a better job with Vietnam than Hubert H. Humphrey.

On Tuesday, August 27 the cousins read that on Monday it had been 95 degrees at 6 P.M. and 90 by 8 P.M.

They read that Joan Baez and Judy Collins did a benefit for Airlift Biafra. They raised $7000.

148

At 2:30 on Channel 12 *One Life to Live* was now up against Channel 7's *Edge of Night*.

A Bill Mauldin cartoon showed two helmeted cops behind barbed wire, bayonets at the ready while reading a headline that said "Democracy Dead in Czechoslovakia." The caption was one cop was saying to the other, "Tsk tsk."

Columnist Russell Baker called Chicago "Stalag '68."

A headline said "Democrats Sailing on a Titanic."

On page seven was an article about women delegates searching for hubby-sitters in Chicago.

The Dow Jones average was down 2.48 to 893.65

The University of Texas Tower clock was to get a cleaning for the first time in thirty years and therefore the observation deck would be closed for a month. There had been ten thousand visitors a month this summer. "No clock," said Michael A. "How we gonna know when it's 10:30 and time for Alfred Hitchcock?"

Tonght's movie on Channel 5 was *Slaughter on Tenth Avenue*.

Two local newspapers, *The Advertiser* and *The Voice* were folding after a four-letter word was found in each in articles on a Killeen Be-in. The articles were the same—a reprint from an East Coast magazine.

Today's quiz told of the swastika being a sun symbol in the ancient East.

According to an Oxford professor, man's inborn instincts fate him to destroy his own species despite human society's advances and technological evolution. "That means the virus is us," Michael A. said.

Today's weather would be the same as yesterday: hot and humid

Neither cousin knew anyone in the four funerals announced in Deaths and Funerals.

They read that, since the establishment of the Texas penal system in 1849, 200 thousand prisoners had been given numbers. The first prisoner was a guy from Lagrange in for cattle theft. A month later the second was a guy from Beaumont who was up for murder.

Late that night on Radio KNOW the cousins learned that Uncle Walter had lost it when Dan Rather was struck by security "thugs" on the convention floor. "So that's where the kaboom is" was Michael A.'s comment.

On Wednesday, August 28, the weather prediction was cloudy with mild nights and hot afternoons. There was a chance of isolated showers with temperatures from 73 to 93.

The cousins read that "HHH" had gotten the presidential nomination on the first ballot, that Dick Nichols, Austin city councilman, was bemoaning something, that there was shooting between government guys and student dissidents outside the presidential palace in Mexico City.

Anita Bryant sang "Happy Birthday" to LBJ—the president was 60 years old. He was in Austin and Anita was at the convention in Chicago.

On Thursday, August 29, the headline was: "Battle Scene Around Hotel." The article by Glen Castlebury of the Capitol staff said that the National Mobilization Committee to End the War in Vietnam had tried to lead a march of 10,000 folks from The Conrad Hilton Hotel to the convention hall but protesters had "laid siege" to the Conrad Hilton. All Texans at the convention again went to bed early—if they went to bed at all—and behind the protection of troops and police as antiwar demonstrators laid siege to the Conrad Hilton for a second night.

Fowler Fare from Wick Fowler: Now the accusations are that the Chicago police clubbed more writers than rioters during the Democratic National Convention.

More Fowler Fare: the average American consumed 3100 calories a day, 500 more than his granpa. Fowler's comment: Yeah, but granpa did more work.

The cousins read that the cops sprayed tear gas and arrested fifty protesters after hundreds rioted against not being able to march. When Michael A. saw a photo of a yippie medic attending a downed comrade, he said:

"That guy sure looks like Taj."

Another photo showed a cameraman waiting for aid after being beaten by cops.

Another photo showed a Latino male being led off by two cops with billy clubs.

Another photo showed third party presidential candidate George Wallace smiling with Mickey Mouse during a tour of Disneyland. Michael A. said, "Is that Ma standing there behind George and Mickey?"

On page 40 a psychologist said inner frustrations can cause hostility. "Do tell," said Jack.

The editorial for that day said a policeman was a symbol whether he liked it or not.

One hundred clergymen marched seven miles to the site of the Democratic National Convention "to express concern on violent suppression of human rights now taking place in Czechoslovakia, Vietnam and Chicago."

So far had 154 protesters had been arrested.

On Thursday, August 29, the paper said it was 91 degrees at 6 P.M. and 84 at 8 P.M. The headline read "Violence in Chicago Debated." Another headline read "Marchers Dispersed With Gas, 79 Arrested." Another read "Wallace Stands With Police."

A photo showed an altered election photo of Mayor Daley with a Hitler mustache.

On Friday, August 30, it was 90 degrees at 6 P.M. and 86 at 8 P.M.

The paper said that Ed Muskie would be HHH's vice presidential choice.

A photo showed protesters trying to push over a paddy wagon.

The Gallup Poll said that 49% of U.S. citizens wanted to return to small town America.

Bill Mauldin's cartoon showed Mayor Richard Daley telling LBJ: "We're taking every precaution to make sure Hubert gets nominated in a free and peaceful atmosphere."

Saturday's paper said that at a Friday press conference Chicago Mayor Richard Daley attempted to explain the police behavior by saying, "The policeman isn't there to create disorder, the policeman is there to preserve disorder." Michael A., of course, had to grin at the mayor's choice of words and say, "Who among us is perfect?"

151

That day Wray Weddell's Austin column said that Wray disapproved of CBS's convention coverage because CBS showed Shirley Maclaine and Rosey Grier thirteen times.

A headline said "Policeman Talks About Violence." The article quoted the policeman as saying, "We're human but we have a job as policemen. And people expect more from a policeman than they would from an ordinary citizen."

There was an article about a weeklong party in Chicago at Hugh Hefner's Playboy Mansion. "Good ol' Hef," said Michael A.

Bill Mauldin's cartoon showed two hippies lying in the street alongside a member of the press. All three were nursing head wounds and one of the hippies was saying to the press guy "Welcome to the Chicago Club."

The paper said that for this coming Tuesday's beginning of school Austin would have fifty thousand students attending thirty-seven schools including two new ones, Crockett High and Walter Prescott Webb Junior High, that there would 2750 teachers which was 213 more than in 1967. "Hurry up an' bring on Zero Population Growth," said Michael A.

A headline said "Offshore Oil, Gas Discovered." The article said that this first discovery by Humble Oil and Refining was twenty-seven miles southeast of Galveston and part of a $600 million federal government lease. "Another stupid human trick" was Michael A.'s analysis.

At 7:30 *Gomer Pyle* was on Channel 7.

At 7:30 *Star Trek* was on San Antonio's Channel 4.

At 8:30 *Hollywood Squares* was on Channel 12.

At 9:30 *Judd for the Defense* was on Channel 12.

At 10:30 the movie on Channel 12 was *The Sleeping City*.

. . .

Saturday evening, August 31, Jack and Michael A. were on the front porch trying to rekindle The Fine Art of Hanging Out in the 60s.

Jack was in Granpa Gage's bentwood rocker reading the Austin paper. Michael A. was beside him in a purple butterfly chair and absorbed by a story in the latest edition of *The Rose in the Gun*.

Between them was the three lock box.

Behind them, Boo Boo was watching from the window of Jack and Jen's bedroom. Boo Boo missed her momma terribly and every time she heard her momma's name, she would go:

"Cheep!"

Jack had read the story about how Texans at the convention had sent their head democrat, John Connally, a telegram urging his delegation to walk out in protest after Dan Rather had been slugged on the convention floor. Jack then read an article about how high birds fly and was about to read about Sealab and how its aquanauts were to live 4300 feet down on the ocean floor near Los Angeles when Michael A. handed him *The Rose in the Gun* and said:

"Check this out."

Below a headline of *Blow by Blow of Lincoln Park Charge by the Chicago Police*, Jack read:

The reporters hid in a dark room overlooking Lincoln Park. Among them were Jean Genet, Terry Southern and William Burroughs reporting for Esquire. *They didn't want to be seen by the police while they watched where the kids had camped out beneath the trees. The pigs were on a ridge beyond. You could make out their baby blue helmets. While waiting for the pigs to charge, the protesters chanted:*

"The whole world is watching, the whole world is watching"

Meanwhile, the reporters were saying how glad they weren't photographers because the photogs were the cops' prime targets. A helicopter came over and shot a searchlight down on the kids: rads and hippies, clean for Gene kids, black and brown militants and those just making the scene.

"If you do not leave the park, you will be subject to arrest," a loudspeaker called in the darkness. It was nearly 12:30 a.m.

The protesters responded by singing "America the Beautiful."

Then it got ugly.

"C'est encroyable," Genet said when he saw the pigs take off their badges and name plates to wade in and charge the kids with billy clubs

swinging madly. Some of the kids countered by throwing bottles and rocks. The reporters called it like a sports event:

"They got another camera guy. Yeah, he's down on the sidewalk."

"Look at that girl with long hair, the one wearing combat boots— she's going up to the fuzz and offering them a yellow rose ... man, that chick's got moxie ... uh-oh, they got her now. Two, no, three cops are on her, one's got her by the hair."

"Uh oh," Jack said.

"Long hair, combat boots," Michael A. said. "That could be Natasha."

"Jen was wearing combat boots when she left here, man, and she had a yellow rose too," Jack said, lowering the paper. "It was probably Jen."

"Cheep!"

Michael A. then reached down between them to pick up the three lock box. "Mayhaps we'll feel better once we recount what's in our piggy bank."

"Cheep!"

. . .

Later on, in the heat of the night of that Saturday, August 31, Ben Jack Gage and his Mexican six string and Miguel Antonio Medina and his brown hollow body Fender bass—and his Slinky—sat on the top step of the front porch. At long last the cousins felt musically inspired from having earlier heard Radio KNOW's Jay Jackson play six new songs from 1968: The Kinks' "Time of the Season", The Stones' "Jumpin Jack Flash", The Beatles' "Lady Madonna", Louis Armstrong's "What a Wonderful World", Jimi Hendrix's "All Along the Watchtower" and Steppenwolf's "Born To Be Wild."

The cousins had been working on Michael A.'s song "Cruisin' for Burgers," but now they were taking a break. Michael A. had just sent the Slinky into its slow motion somersault down the steps and the five kittens were stalking it while Boo Boo watched.

Jack stood up and walked over to take a pee off the east end of the porch. While peeing, he said, "Whaddya think ol' Taj will do if

154

he gets 30 billion for the bees'n hummingbirds? Start the Republic of Tajmania?"

"Actually, a sovereign nation's not a bad idea," Michael A. said. "Walks In Blue Green claims his Rez is a sovereign nation."

"Hmmm," Jack said as he sat down again, "sure would be cool to pee off our front porch some distant eve in the Republic of Tajmania."

"Taj is a good guy to have liking you … and now I'm liking him even more."

"Mighty big of you, Cuz," Jack said, "and I sincerely mean that."

By now the Slinky was motionless at the bottom of the steps and the five kittens and Boo Boo had begun roaming the front yard.

Michael A. said, "'Look to the past for lessons and the future for answers'—'why do the heathen rage and the people imagine a vain thing?'" Then with a shrug he answered the question, saying, "'Cause familiarity breeds contempt.'"

Jack nodded and said, "Like Nacho always says, 'I don't pick the sunset an' I don't choose the sunrise—"

"'I just live out my days an' breathe through my nights.'"

"'I die each day or I live a little—the choice is mine.'"

"'The main aim is to amuse yourself'," Michael A. said, grinning. "That's from Oscar Wilde."

"'Live long and prosper'," Jack said, also grinning. "That's from that new TV show *Star Trek.*"

"*Star Trek* was on Channel 4 this very night," Michael A. said.

"Shoot, we missed it."

"It's a good show for the virus that is us because it offers hope—one planet, one world!"

"Michael A., how come you'n Nacho call us humans a virus?"

"On account of a virus is the species in nature we humans resemble the most."

The cousins then paused as a caravan of honking cars filled with young people drove by going west on 19th Street. "The students are back," Jack said. "Are you goin' back to school? Fall semester registration begins September 17."

"School's not a very providential undertaking for me right now since, besides family biz, September 17 is when Purple People Eater Productions will resume showing movies in Batts Auditorium. For your viewing pleasure that night the feature will be *The Wild One* starring Marlon Brando and Lee Marvin."

"Cool." Nodding. "A back to school special."

"And, unlike a Love-In, it is a tried and truly providential venture." Then: "What about you? Are you goin' back to school?"

"I got no choice. These days a fella needs a good lawyer or a lyin' shrink to stay free of the draft." Then Jack winked and said, "Or a death certificate. And that takes money. Which is why I'm all for us bein' such a goin'n growin' concern in the underground economy."

"Michael A. said, "We're gonna shoot lightning through the sky with what Nacho brought us in the *Zak Be*."

Confused now, Jack frowned and said, "Yucatecan honey'n chanclas?"

"Nope. Nacho calls it 'Panama Red.'"

"Whoa! Nobody tells me nothin' til it' a done deal."

"None of us knew our brand of hippie capitalism's goin' nation-wide," Michael A. said. "We're steppin' up'n out."

"Oh, well," Jack said with a shrug of acceptance.

"You think we could start our own country, Jack?"

"Why not? It very well could be that in these dizzying days the time is right for the Republic of Tajmania."

A record player in the Gamma Sig house now began to play Johnny Cash's "Folsom Prison Blues", the live version Cash had recorded in January, 1968, at California's Folsom Prison. After listening some, Jack sighed and said:

"One thing we durn sure better not do is mention much of what we're doin' or we'll land in the Big House with Uncle Tunoose."

"Loose lips sink ships, no risks, no riches—caca pasa, chachalaca."

"How's Uncle Tunoose doin' down there anyway?"

"Three hots'n a cot an' he's studying sociology—talismans of the leisure class an' conspicuous consumption an' all like that."

Jack said, "And planned obsolescence too, I betcha—which is why you'n me is both drivin' vehicles that're twenty years old."

"Cool Breeze's pink Caddy does seem to suit me, does it not?" Then Michael A. got a sly grin and said, "Ahhh, but I got no stage presence."

Jack said, "Life is change"—sighing—"and also absurd juxtaposition."

"Just as long as it ain't planned obsolescence," Michael A. said. Then: "So how's live-in love treating you anyway?"

"Whuuut 'live-in love?' She ain't here. Jen's off someplace, somewhere in a war zone." Then, his tone more serene: "But love is wild, love is real."

"*I* wanta know if love is wild," Michael A. said, his mind on Signe, Two Moons and Li Mam, Graciela, too. Then, thinking aloud: "'Some distant eve' ... 'someplace, somewhere' ... sometime ago—sounds downright lyrical, don't it?" He was beginning to finger frets on his Fender next ... when a door slammed shut from within the house and Michael A. quickly got to his feet.

"Let's git"— his tone hushed—"Mona's out an' about."

Jack chuckled again. "Where we gonna go?"

"Let's have a short beer at this bar I been meanin' ta show ya, a little dive what's lately been interestin' my commercial mind."

"A dive, huh? I like dives—where's this 'un?"

"801 Red River." Next, as across 19th Street on a stereo in the Gamma Sig house, Janis now began singing "Summertime," Michael A. said, "The way I see it, this bar is the next stop on the Road for us fellow travelers."

. . .

Tres said, "And it was Michael A. who wanted to buy 801 Red River?"

"It was his vision, his idea, yes, by way of Purple People Eater Productions and Xutan Partners. Same with the 19th Street house."

"Sounds like Michael A. was kind of like Taj—a good guy to have liking you."

Jen put on her granny glasses and said, "I should tell you about the time Michael A. rolled over in bed and found himself in the porn industry." Then she looked in her lap at another of the weathered black-and-white snapshots with curled-up corners. The snapshot was from Jolinda Biggs' second photo shoot of the band, the first set of photos ever taken of Que Tal. The photo had been taken in August, 1968, at the 19th Street house. It showed six members of the band lined up in one behind the other on the steps leading up to the front porch. On the bottom step was Jen flanked by Wiley and Beep Beep. Behind Jen were Natasha, Taj, Michael A., Ben Jack and Cool Breeze.

Tres now said, "So for you the '60s began when your father pulled the rug out from you on April 16, 1962, and they ended with the Democratic National Convention at the end of August in 1968?"

"Yes, and that was the worst end to the best of times," she said, sounding tired. "What we did in Chicago was an act of altruism. I myself had resolved that I had to do something, anything, to stand up and be counted after RFK's assassination in June of '68 ... when I showed my moxie by offering that rose to those cops what I got for my nonviolence was violence. I was roughed up ... I was struck in the abdomen with a billy club and in the paddy wagon I lost the baby. If Taj had not been there, I might have bled to death."

"I never knew that you had a miscarriage, Gram."

"I never cried, I never shed a tear, I never ..." After a sigh she said, "Well, suffice to say that, coming so soon after having Stetson hats with shotguns put hate in my heart at the Hill on the Moon, those baby blue riot helmets with billy clubs in Chicago finished off my idealism and completed my radicalization ... but that was then and this is now ... what's done is done, no more bereavement, all tears are the same." After another sigh, she said, "So, yes, it is my belief, my feeling, that the conflict in and around Lincoln Park the last week in August of 1968 effected the beginning of the end for the idealism of the 1960s ... the end of innocence ... life is change and change is life."

"Life is compromise."

"So say la maya." Then Jen leaned back in her bentwood rocker to compose herself before saying, "I hope what I've been telling you doesn't sound like my memoirs."

158

"Well, in a way it's like you said earlier—'a romantic reminiscence.' It's also a tale of a renaissance, a personal account of rising times—but mostly it's history."

"So be it. Years like 1968 don't come around very often ... and we were there."

"For the best of times and the worst of times. Yeah, it's quite a tale, Gram—Walks in Beauty and Like the Night, Bridge Beyond the Light and Dawn Song, Marvin, Cool Breeze and Dancing Lightning."

"And don't forget our Maya Karma and Tiny Dancer." Then, sounding even more tired: "Life in prison."

Tres hung his head in the silence that followed. It was an awkward moment and one that again made Tres think that his grandmother might cry. When he reached out and took her hand, Jen turned away and looked outside. She would not look at him, even when he said, "Life in prison is tough when it's one of your own, Gram."

"I get chills up and down my spine talking about the old days," she said. "And there are other things besides Mona that will never be answered ... you know, we always thought that our old daykeeper had a hand in Taj finding his voice ... we also thought Cool Breeze might have been murdered." Then:

"Wouldn't you like to know more about your mom? My side of the story?"

Acknowledgements

In memory of those now gone from the Austin scene, including but not limited to (in no order)—Elyssa Llast, Jackson Boyette, "Young Dave" Moran, Ike Ritter, T. J. "Tiny" McFarland, D. K. Little, Danny Carmichael, Dick Knudsen, George Vizard, Benny Thurman, Stacy Sutherland, Doyle Bramhall, Keith Ferguson, Uncle John Turner, Rusty Wier, Kenneth Threadgill, Cody Hubach, Blind George, Nick Travis III, Traci Lamar Hancock, Pia Ramos, E.R. Shorts, Joseph William "Pinetop" Perkins, Ken Cottrell, Alex Napier, Townes Van Zandt, Jesse "Guitar" Taylor, Jimmy Carl Black, Danny Turansky, Freddie Pharoah, Tyler Dee "T.D." Bell, and Stevie Ray Vaughan.

And with special thanks to our living friends—to Roger "One Knite" Collins—what fun pickin' his brain—and to Liz Henry. And to SJ Barba and Sal De Jesus for all of their support.

www.ingramcontent.com/pod-product-compliance
Lightning Source LLC
Chambersburg PA
CBHW051301250626
47155CB00009B/3390